The Story of John Wesley's Sisters, or

Seven Sisters in Search of Love

by

FREDERICK E. MASER

To

Mary Louise, my wife,
Without whose help and
encouragement I probably
wouldn't do anything.

The Story of
John Wesley's Sisters, or
Seven Sisters in Search of Love

by

FREDERICK E. MASER

Academy Books

Rutland, Vermont

ISBN 0-914960-68-7
Library of Congress Catalog Card No. 88-081533
Fourth Printing

The Story of John Wesley's Sisters

Printed and Bound in the United States of America
by Academy Books, Rutland, VT 05701-0757

Contents

Reference Abbreviations

This volume uses the newest technique for documenting its facts. The following abbreviations refer to the books relied upon for reference; and they are placed at appropriate points in the text. The general reader may ignore them. The scholar, seeking the exact reference, may check the abbreviation in the text with the list compiled here and quickly find the documentation from which a particular statement was taken.

Bos	Boswell, James. *The Life of Samuel Johnson,* 3 vols. London: J. M. Dent & Co. New York: McClure, Phillips & Co., 1901.
Clarke	Clarke, Adam. *Memoirs of the Wesley Family.* London: J. Kershaw, 1823.
C&M	Dr. Coke and Mr. Moore. *The Life of The Rev. John Wesley.* London: G. Paramore 1792.
CWJ	Jackson, Thomas. *The Journal of the Rev. Charles Wesley.* 2 vols. London: John Mason, 1849.
DW	Wright, Dudley. *The Epworth Phenomena.* London: William Rider & Son, 1917.
ED, *FC*	Edwards, Maldwyn. *Family Circle.* London: Epworth Press, 1949.
Green	Green, V.H.H. *The Young Mr. Wesley.* London: Edward Arnold, Ltd., 1961.
Harmon	Harmon, Rebecca Lamar. *Susanna Mother of the Wesleys.* Nashville, New York: Abingdon Press, 1968.
Heit, *BI*	Heitzenrater, Richard P. *Diary of an Oxford Methodist, Benjamin Ingham,* 1733-1734. Durham: Duke University Press, 1985.
Heit, *MWM*	Heitzenrater, Richard P. *Mary Wesley's Marriage.* In the *Proceedings of the Wesley Historical Society.* Vol. XL. October 1976.
JWJ	Curnock, Nehemiah. *The Journal of the Rev. John Wesley.* 8 Vols. London: Epworth Press, 1938.

JWL   Wesley, John. Letters, Vol. I and II; Vol. 25 and 26 in *The Bicentennial Edition of the Works of John Wesley*. Nashville: Abingdon Press, 1980.

JWLT   Telford, John. *The Letters of the Rev. John Wesley*. 8 Vols. London: Epworth Press, 1931.

Stev.   Stevenson, George J. *Memorials of the Wesley Family*. London: S. W. Partridge. New York: Nelson and Phillips, (1876)

Ty, *OM*   Tyerman, The Rev. L. *The Oxford Methodists*. New York: Harper and Brothers, 1873.

Ty, *SW*   Tyerman, The Rev. L. *The Life and Times of the Rev. Samuel Wesley*. London: Simpkin, Marshall & Co., 1866.

JOHN WESLEY RESCUED FROM THE FIRE.

The Wesley family escaping from the Rectory fire.

Chapter One

Introduction

This book is about the strange, tragic, though at times happy experiences of the seven sisters of John and Charles Wesley, the founders of Methodism, one of the largest Protestant denominations in the world today.

Anyone with the slightest knowledge of religious history has heard of John and Charles Wesley. John influenced eighteenth century England, and every generation since his death in 1791, by his evangelistic preaching and his organization of what later became the British Methodist Church in England *Plus other Methodist denominations* and the United Methodist Church in America. Charles, his brother, wrote over nine thousand hymns and poems, many of which are still sung in Christian churches today. Their father and mother, Samuel and Susanna Wesley, likewise etched their names deeply in Methodism's hall of fame.

However, few people are aware that John and Charles Wesley had an elder brother, Samuel, Jr., and seven sisters, who reached maturity. In addition, there were nine other brothers and sisters who did not survive their infancy.

If the sisters had not been over-shadowed by their talented and highly educated brothers some of them, at least, might have received the recognition they deserved. Emilia or "Emily," the eldest sister, was especially gifted in music appreciation and poetry. Her brother, John, said that she was the best reader of John Milton he had ever heard. Another sister, Mehetable or "Hetty" wrote poetry of sufficient merit to have had some of her work published in a variety of household magazines as well as in *The Gentleman's Magazine*, a prestigious publication of eighteenth-century England. Martha, known as "Patty," became a close friend of Samuel Johnson, the famous eighteenth century lexicographer, who invited her to live in his house along with two other women for whom he was providing. Anne or "Nancy" married a well-to-do land surveyor. Susanna, called "Sukey," married a wealthy land owner; Mary or "Molly," married a clergyman; and Kezia or "Kezzy," the youngest sister, died before her talents were fully developed. None of the sisters received a formal education. Only the three brothers graduated from Oxford.

This does not mean, however, that the Wesleys spent every possible penny on the education of their three sons and failed completely to provide for their daughters. It is true none of the sisters attended boarding schools or were furnished tutors or governesses. However, the education provided by their own parents probably surpassed any training the sisters might have received from disinterested teachers.

Susanna, their mother, began the education of the sisters when they were only five years old by teaching them their letters in one day. She had to spend a day and a half with Mary or "Molly" and with Anne or "Nancy" causing her to think, for a time, that they were exceedingly dull. She then followed a strict routine for the further education of all her children. As a result of this training each of the sisters, except Kezzy, could read better in a short time "than the most of women can do as long as they live." (JWJ, III, p. 37)

Samuel, their father, taught Mehetabel or "Hetty" Latin and Greek. He also added his vast erudition to the instructions given by his wife to his other daughters and sons.

This was a laudable and exceptional practice in eighteenth century England where as important a statesman as the Marquis of Lansdowne once said, "Women are domestic animals and should never be taught to go from home." (ED, *FC*, p. 134) He believed as did many eighteenth century educators, that women of his class needed only to learn about spinning and some moral precepts to make them fully desirable as wives, their chief purpose for living. He was advocating what later was allegedly expressed by a Kentucky hillbilly, "Keep 'em barefoot, pregnant, and in the kitchen!"

In spite of their poverty, caused more by Samuel's mismanagement than by his lack of an adequate salary, the Wesleys had a small staff of servants. This gave Mrs. Wesley the leisure to supervise the education of her entire family and to direct their activities.

All of the sisters engaged in love affairs. Some of these were glossed over by the historians of the Wesley family with rhetoric that concealed rather than revealed what actually occurred. In addition, the sisters may have had more lovers than those for which there is documentary evidence. A clue to this possibility may be deduced from a remark attributed to Samuel Wesley, Sr. at the time the family was seeking an explanation for the strange rappings, groanings and levitations caused by a supposed ghost whom Emily, the eldest sister, nicknamed "Old Jeffrey."

"Old Jeffrey" haunted the rectory from December 1716 through January 1717, and in a less vigorous manner for about the next three months. The phenomenon began when one of the maids heard a dismal noise at the dining room door like the groaning of one expiring. She was laughed at by the sisters and Mrs. Wesley until several members of the family heard similar sounds in various parts of the house. When the phenomena became more frequent they were reported to the Rev. Mr. Wesley, himself.

Emily Wesley stated that on hearing about the ghost, her father

> smiled and gave no answer, but was more careful than usual, from that time, to see us in bed, imagining it to be some of us young women, that sat up late and made a noise. His incredulity, and especially his imputing it to us, or our lovers, made me, I own, desirous of its continuance till he was convinced. (DW, p. 25)

The gloomy attic where, at her father's command, a very frightened teen-ager—Anne Wesley—blew on a horn in an attempt to scare away "Old Jeffrey," the ghost that was haunting Epworth Rectory (see pages 72, 73).

At this time Emily was about twenty-four, Susanna about twenty-one, Mary nearer twenty, Mehetable nineteen, Anne about fourteen or fifteen, Martha ten and Kezzy, the youngest, about six. Obviously, the older sisters might well have been meeting with lovers at night whom they did not want connected with the noises lest these visits be stopped. At any rate, the rector thought it wise to notice more particularly if his daughters were carrying on some secret meetings, and he began to check their bedtimes more carefully. When he, himself, heard the noises and was forceably shoved against the wall by the supposed poltergeist, he seems to have forgotten about his daughters' lovers.

As they matured each of the sisters and brothers developed a strong, independent spirit. Even the cruelest experiences with their lovers or their husbands or with other members of their own family, were unable to break this spirit of independence. The Wesleys were a close-knit family but they were not always in harmony. They interfered with one another's lives and loves and often wrought havoc by their actions. Nevertheless, each manifested his or her own independence and managed to survive the most dismal circumstances. In general, the Wesleys were survivors.

Samual Wesley, Sr. was at first a Dissenter but later became an Anglican priest. However, he never lost the influence of his Puritan background. He served, for a time, as a Chaplain at sea, and later at a small parish in London. He married in London and had his first child, Samuel, Jr., before accepting a living at South Ormsby. Three of his daughters were born here besides three other children who did not survive. His stern Puritan nature is reflected in an incident in his parish as told by John Wesley:

> The Marquis of Normanby had a house in the parish of South Ormsby, where a woman who lived with him usually resided. This lady *would* be intimate with my mother, whether *she* would or not. To such an intercourse my father would not submit. Coming in one day, and finding this intrusive visitant sitting with my mother, he went up to her, took her by the hand, and very fairly handed her out. The nobleman resented the affront so outrageously, as to make it necessary for my father to resign the living. (Ty, *SW*, p. 198)

According to later researchers, Wesley here is wrong in several facts. The woman ushered out by Wesley's father was not the mistress of the Marquis of Normanby but of the Earl of Castleton who had rented a house for her. In addition, Samuel Wesley continued to have a satisfactory relationship with the Marquis, himself, who, later in life, helped Samuel financially. The real patrons of the parish, furthermore, were the members of the Massingberd family, and the likelihood of Samuel having been forced to resign his parish is probably an exaggeration. (Ty, *SW*, note on p. 467)

However, the incident clearly reveals Samuel Wesley's puritanical attitude toward the rather permissive style of living common among the upper classes in the late seventeenth and eighteenth centuries. It also helps to explain his later attitude toward his daughters, especially toward Hetty.

Samuel Wesley moved to Epworth early in 1697 and served the parish — to which Wroot was later added — for almost thirty-nine years. During this time the remaining of his total of nineteen children were born. Three boys and seven girls grew to maturity.

A curious fact about the seven sisters is that not a single picture of any of them is in existence today.* There are numerous portraits, paintings and engravings of Samuel, Jr., Charles and John, and pictures also of their parents Susanna and Samuel, Sr., but none of any of the sisters. Picture-taking was

---

* An artist's conception of Mrs Hall (Martha Wesley) appears on page 115 Vol. one of Walter Thornbury's work *Old and New London* . . . published by Cassell, Potter, and Galpin, London, Paris and New York. (N.D.) Mrs Hall is seated on the right of the picture as she attends a tea party at the home of Samual Johnson the famed 18th Century lexicographer. See illustration in this volume.

From OLD AND NEW LONDON
by Walter Thornbury

Courtesy of Bryn Mawr
College Library

Martha Wesley (Mrs. Westley Hall) stirs her tea as she converses with Samuel Johnson (center) at a party at Bolt Court. James Boswell holds his chin in his hand as he concentrates to remember every word of Johnson's remarks.

not a common practice in the eighteenth century. The camera was not invented until a later date, and generally, only the rich or distinguished had portraits painted of themselves or engravings made to record their features. Written descriptions, furthermore, are not always a safe guide to the appearance of a person. Martha, one of the sisters who lived a few months longer than her brother, John, and was buried in the same vault, was thought to resemble him to the point that had she dressed as a man she might well have passed for her short-statured brother. Since John taught his sister to write, she even wrote like him. James Boswell, the biographer of Samuel Johnson, gives us an entirely different picture of her when he writes, "lean, lank, preaching Mrs. Hall (Martha Wesley) . . ." (BOS, *LJ*, III, p. 162) If she looked like her brother she could hardly have been thought of as "lanky." However, words have different meanings for different persons, and the general opinion of scholars is that Martha strongly resembled her brother, John.

Martha was the only sister who kept any kind of a journal, and not many of the letters of the sisters are extant. This may be due to a variety of circumstances. In 1709 a fire destroyed the rectory and nearly all the personal property of the Wesleys. Later several of the sisters lived for a time with their father's brother, known as "Uncle Matthew." Emily served as a teacher in Lincoln and later for a Mrs. Taylor, where she was joined by Kezzy. Emily later opened her own school at Gainsborough. Hetty and Martha served as governesses and companions in the home of the Granthams at Kelstein. In fact, the sisters moved about more than one would expect.

Although moving from one place to another may inspire the writing of letters to relatives, informing them of daily happenings, it is not usually conducive to the storing of records and papers. In addition, since one of the Wesley sisters became pregnant out of wedlock and several of the sisters had very unhappy love affairs, they would not be inclined to keep the letters relative to these grievous events. Furthermore, John and Charles Wesley were constantly travelling and would not be likely to save the letters from their sisters unless they were suitable for publication. John saved some of the letters of his sisters, but not many.

John Wesley comments on another peculiarity of the sisters, namely, that they did not assist him much in his work of Methodism. This is not entirely accurate. Several of the sisters professed a religious experience typical of the Methodists, and, for some years, Emily did the work of a deaconess in West Street Chapel, London; but beyond this and a few other trivial activities the sisters were not avid Methodists. This seems strange since the sisters, in their youth had adored their brother, John, and Kezzy was very close to Charles, nursing him through a serious illness. However, their adoration did not seem to spill over into the Methodist movement. They were busy about their own affairs which centered for the most part, in their various lovers, husbands, families, and other personal matters. Methodism naturally took a second

From OLD AND NEW LONDON
by Walter Thurnbury

Courtesy of Bryn Mawr
College Library

Bolt Court where Samuel Johnson entertained many 18th century celebrities and where he also entertained Martha Wesley (Mrs. Westley Hall).

place. They were more *indifferent* to Methodism rather than *actively oppos-ed* to it as was also their eldest brother, Samuel, Jr. Methodism either motivated persons to Methodist activity by its persuasive doctrines of God's love for all humankind or it repelled them by its misunderstood claims to Christian perfection. It did neither for the Wesley sisters. Maybe they were too close to its founders to be either overawed by its doctrines or repulsed by its seemingly arrogant claims. Emily, on one occasion, wrote a tart letter to John Wesley about his ideas on confession, but the other sisters seldom entered into any controversy with him or aided him much in spreading his doctrines. At any rate, Methodism today draws little inspiration from the examples of the Wesley sisters.

On the other hand, one can more readily empathize with the Wesley sisters than with either John or Charles Wesley or their parents. The sisters faced all the different kinds of frustrations, heartaches, poverty, despair, happiness, triumphs and defeats characteristic of the television soap operas today. One of the sisters — Hetty — was forced into a loveless marriage by her father after he discovered she was pregnant with the child of another lover who had deserted her. Martha and Kezia were wooed at the same time by Westley Hall, one of John Wesley's colleagues and a member of his Holy Club. After Hall finally married Martha, Kezia came to live with the happy couple. A fourth sister — Molly — was a cripple, probably from a fall in her infancy. She became the family jest and an object of derision in the community. However, she fell in love with a young student who assisted her father in his scholarly work on the book of Job. They were happily married for a year when Molly died in childbirth. Another sister was the victim of wife abuse.

One author has labelled the lives of the sisters "a matter for tears," (ED, *FC*, p. 132) and most authors have dismissed the sisters with a paragraph or two. Few have sought to bring them to life or to place them on the stage in Epworth, Wroot or London as human beings rather than as minor actors playing insignificant roles. Yet, almost all the Wesley sisters led the kind of lives out which drama is born.

A third strange fact about the Wesley family was its lack of love. The family was well organized by the efficient supervision of Susanna; each member was imbued with a love for learning and a deep respect for religion, particularly Anglicanism; and each member was taught to obey his or her parents and, as far as conscience permitted, to honor the King. Members of the family were expected to be loyal to one another and, if possible, to help one another. There was a unity about the Wesley family that was com-mendable, but it was not a unity cemented by love.*

---

* Most authorities will probably disagree with me at this point. After reading the story of the seven sisters, of course, each person is entitled to make up his or her own mind. One deciding question might be whether or not the reader would have wanted to have been a member of the Wesley household.

Susanna had a remarkable grasp upon a philosophical concept of love. She wrote a lengthy letter to her son, Samuel, revealing an amazing fund of knowledge and understanding. She sees in love "a desire to please and a desire to obey"; (Stev, p. 181) but she writes little about that warm human relationship that makes two hearts beat as one. She lists the virtues as "prudence, justice, temperance, and fortitude." To these she adds "magnanimity, magnificence, liberality, modesty, gentleness, courtesy, truth and urbanity," but she does not include charity or love. (Stev, p. 177)

Some may object to my analysis by arguing the virtues she lists combine to express love; and yet a person may possess all of these virtues and still lack the warmth of personality, and the willingness to forget oneself in a profound, compulsive desire to unite with other souls in an expression of true love.

Possibly each member of the family unknowingly felt this lack. John constantly pleaded for the love of his mother. In an early letter he changed his conclusion from "Your dutiful Son" to the expression "Your Affectionate, Dutiful Son." His mother replied:

Dear J[acky], the conclusion of your letter is very kind, that you were ever dutiful I very well know, but I know myself enough to rest satisfied with a moderate share of your affection. Indeed it would be unjust of me to desire the love of anyone. Your prayers I want and wish; nor shall I cease while I live to beseech Almighty God to bless you! Adieu! (JWL, I, p. 218)

Her kindness is self evident; her virtue and her concern for her children are unquestioned; but her lack of love is equally apparent.

Maybe it is expecting too much of a woman who has borne nineteen children, supervised the education of ten of them, provided for their comfort while, at the same time, serving and controlling an irascible husband, to give her family that love for which they longed. Susanna was a practical woman and not particularly emotional. It was probably only in her old age that she began to appreciate fully the meaning of love and, herself, long for the security provided by a loving relationship. Nor should this be surprising. The eighteenth century, in which she lived, was the age of reason. Emotions, however deeply felt, were not easily expressed or popularly recognized and approved.

On the other hand, Samuel Wesley, Sr., who is usually considered to have been stern and forbidding, expressed his love for his sons at least, in a manner that is surprising in an eighteenth century father.

It was not unusual for him to end his letters with an expression of deep affection. Once he wrote "Naught else but blessing from your loving father." On another occasion he said, "However, nothing shall be wanting to make it so that lies in the power of your loving father." Or he might simply write, "from your loving father." (JWL, Letters I, pp. 223-229 and other places)

From an old print.

Epworth Church as it may have appeared in the 18th Century when the Wesley sisters occupied its pews on a Sunday to hear their father preach.

It is doubtful if he addressed his daughters in similar terms of endearment. None of his daughters seemed particularly fond of him.

Nevertheless, as we shall see, the need for love was evident in the lives of the Wesley sisters. They vied with each other to secure the respect, appreciation and especially the affection and love of their brothers as well as their parents. Each of them also sought for love outside the family circle, usually unsuccessfully. In short, the Wesley sisters sought at least one thing from life—namely, love. How they went about their search for love and whether or not they found it, is the theme of this slim volume on SEVEN SISTERS IN SEARCH OF LOVE!

In closing this brief introduction, the author wishes to express appreciation of the work of Dr. Frank Baker, Editor of the Wesley Works Project of which only a few volumes have so far been published. However, among these have been two volumes of the letters of John Wesley which Dr. Baker has judiciously interspersed with numerous important letters from John Wesley's parents, his two brothers, his sisters, and others.

Dr. Richard Heitzenrater, probably the leading Wesleyan scholar today, has very kindly read this manuscript making many wise and helpful suggestions and corrections. He is now at work on the diaries of John Wesley which, when they are finally published through the Wesley Works Project, will provide the most useful primary source for John Wesley's life and times. He was recently elected General Editor of the Project.

The author is also greatly indebted to *Memoirs of the Wesley Family* by Adam Clarke and *Memorials of the Wesley Family* by George J. Stevenson. Both of these nineteenth century authorities published many of the letters of the sisters and preserved some of the traditions surrounding them.

The numerous biographers of John and Charles Wesley have served as invaluable though not always accurate sources for information about the Wesley sisters. Particularly helpful have been Maldwyn Edwards' entertaining book *Family Circle* and Mrs. Nolan Harmon's slim volume on *Susanna, Mother of the Wesleys. The Young Mr. Wesley* by Dr. Vivian H. H. Green has also proved useful since it relies, to some extent, on certain of the unpublished diaries.

All these sources, however, with the exception of those in the Wesley Works Project, must be used with appropriate caution. Nevertheless, it is sometimes difficult to unravel the sequence of events in the lives of the sisters and their husbands, especially when authorities differ.

Chapter Two

Heartbreak and Healing
The Story of Emilia Wesley
Mrs. Robert Harper

Childhood and Youth

Emilia Wesley or "Emily" as she was generally called, was, in her childhood and youth, a happy, contented person whose laughter was like the sound of muted bells. She was probably born on the last day of the Year 1692. On January 13th, 1693 she was baptised by her father, the rector of the small church dedicated to St. Leonard at South Ormsby near Louth, where the Tennysons received their schooling. She was the third child of her parents. Her older sister, Susanna, died about three and one-half months after Emily was born, and her parents naturally concentrated their affection upon her and her brother, Samuel, Jr., who had been born in 1690. Their attachment to Samuel, Jr. and Emily must have become even more pronounced when the next two children — twins named Annesley and Jedidiah — died; one before he was two months old and one when he was about 14 months old.

The South Ormsby rectory was not necessarily the most healthful place to live, although the deaths of three infants would not have been uncommon in eighteenth century England with its high rate of infant mortality. The rectory seems to have been little more than a small hut in a town of about thirty-six houses and a church with its tower, nave, chancel and a small chapel on the north side. There was also a gentleman's seat, the Hall, surrounded by a park which gave the town a pleasing aspect. However, Samuel Wesley, Sr., Emily's father, described the rectory as

. . . a mean cot, composed of reeds and clay, (Ty, *SW*, p. 128)

We do not know how many rooms comprised the house, but before Samuel Wesley, Sr. moved to the living at Epworth, Lincolnshire, in 1697, his household probably consisted of four children, his wife and himself, with possibly a servant or two. Susanna or "Sukey" had been born in 1695, and Mary or "Molly" the following year.

It was at Epworth that Mrs. Wesley, with the help of her husband, began a strict routine for the education of her family. She and her husband were both highly intelligent and well educated according to the standards of the time. Samuel was an Oxford graduate, Susanna was the brilliant daughter of an equally brilliant dissenting clergyman. She was sufficiently versed in theology to have seriously considered embracing Socinianism. Among other beliefs, Socinianism was opposed to the doctrine of the Trinity and the atonement. Later, under the influence of Samuel, who was then a student and a friend, she was led to a more orthodox theology. Eventually, after analyzing the doctrinal differences between the Dissenters and the Anglicans, she became a professing member of the Church of England.

The couple probably dreamed of the day when their son, Samuel, Jr. would be an Oxford graduate. Although they had no plans for sending their daughters to expensive boarding schools, they hoped, themselves, to train them to become governesses, one of the few positions open to the women of that day. Young Emily must have gladdened their hearts by her quick response to their efforts toward her education. She was instructed by her parents along with her brother, Samuel, Jr., and she read constantly. Her extant letters are written in a clear, round hand that suggests an aptitude for learning. However, her life soon became more complicated by family affairs.

It would be an understatement to say that Samuel and Susanna were a prolific couple, but it would account for the fact that Emily soon found herself surrounded by a brood of brothers and sisters whom she helped to rear. Mehetable or "Hetty" was born in 1697, the year the Wesleys moved to Epworth; Anne or "Nancy" was probably born in 1701; John or "Jacky" was born in 1703; Martha or "Patty" about 1706; Charles probably in the following year; and Kezia or "Kezzy," the youngest, probably in 1710. In between these and other births, nine children were born who did not survive their infancy. In all, Susanna gave birth to nineteen children in a little more than twenty years.

It is an amazing fact that ten of the family reached maturity. Death was almost a way of life in the eighteenth century, and in many families few or none of the children survived beyond infancy or early childhood. Mrs. Wesley wrote to her son John from Wroot on September 10th, 1724:

> The smallpox has been very mortal at Epworth most of this summer. Our family have all had it besides me, and I hope God will preserve me from it, because your father can't yet very well spare money to bury me. (JWL, I, p. 149)

It is a strange reason for hoping for recovery, but there was a better one. The household needed the firm hand of Susanna to direct its strict routine. Each child was assigned various tasks and each helped the next younger one with his or her studies. Study was a requirement, not an elective, in the Wesley household.

In addition, the parents of the Wesleys placed a tremendous emphasis on religion and the importance of piety and a virtuous life. In 1710 Susanna wrote a long letter to her son, Samuel, who was about to matriculate at Oxford University. What she wrote here she probably had taught many times in her household school:

> . . . How many persons on a deathbed have bitterly bewailed the sins
> of their past life, and made large promises of amendment if it would
> have pleased God to have spared them; but none that ever lived, or died,
> repented a course of piety and virtue. Then why should you not improve
> the experience of those who have gone before you, . . . have a good
> courage, eternity is at hand. (Stev, p. 237)

Emily became a good classical scholar. She developed an appreciative
ear for music and poetry and, according to her brother, John, her reading
of Milton was a sheer delight to hear.

She seems to have had free access to her father's library, and, one day
while her father was in London, she found a book describing the labors of
two Danish missionaries at Tranquebar. She became interested in the volume,
took it to her mother who asked Emily to read it to her. Mrs. Wesley was
deeply impressed by the account. She knew she, herself, could never become
a missionary, but she resolved to take especial care in the religious training
of her family and those of the community whom she could reach. As for
her children, she set aside a certain time each week when she could hold a
private conversation with each child separately. The custom was probably
one of the chief means by which she knit her family to her. Emily and Martha,
or "Patty," were especially impressed and were strongly linked to her by the
deepest emotional ties. John also was impressed by the custom, and later
in life begged his mother to pray for him during the hour of the week in
which she had formerly conversed with him.

Though Emily was probably not so beautiful as some of her sisters, she
was, nevertheless, well proportioned, with a pleasant, wholesome appearance,
her cheeks only slightly reddened by the cold of the Epworth winters and
the warm sun of the summers. She was not an outdoors person. She usually
stayed at home as did most of the Wesley children. Their parents were not
social snobs. They simply did not think the children of their rough parishoners
would prove suitable playmates. Furthermore, there was work, study and
play to occupy all of their children's time. Emily became a second mother
to the Wesley brood and summarized her own life by writing:

> . . . I lived easy . . . having most necessaries, though few diversions,
> and never going abroad. Yet after working all day I read some pleasant
> book at night, and was contented enough; . . . (Stev, p. 263)

In addition, the Wesleys in these early years amused themselves by playing cards and, under the watchful eye of Susanna, received lessons from a
dancing master. Later in life, John Wesley, himself, attests to this fact in
a letter to James Barry October 1, 1773;

> My mother never would suffer one of her children to 'go to a dancing
> school'. But she had a dancing master come to her house who taught

all of us what was sufficient *in her presence.* (JWLT, VI, p. 47)

After John left for Oxford his visits home were eagerly anticipated by his sisters. They would go berry hunting or in search of flowers. Sometimes they visited a few chosen neighbors and at other times John would read aloud to his sisters from the plays of Scarron or the poems of Lewis.

Beyond these activities each of the sisters was assigned a share of the family chores. Years later, Samuel, Jr., in a delightful poem sent to his sister "Hetty," harkened back to some of the household activities of his sisters:

> The spacious glebe around the house
> Affords full pasture to the cows,
> Whence largely milky nectar flows
>   O sweet and cleanly dairy!
> Unless or Moll, or Anne, or you,
> Your duty should neglect to do,
> And then 'ware haunches black and blue
>   By pinching of a fairy.
>
> . . . .
> Observe the warm, well littered sty,
> Where sows and pigs and porklets lie;
> Nancy or you the draff supply;
>   They swill and care not whither.
>
> . . . but not so glad
> As you to wait upon your dad!
>   Oh 'tis exceeding pretty!
> Methinks I see you striving all
> Who first shall answer to his call,
> Or lusty Anne, or feeble Moll,
>   Sage Pat, or sober Hetty. (Stev, p. 327)

Emily is not directly mentioned in the poem, probably because she was so much older than her sisters, and her duties were more in relation to her mother and often as a mother.

Emily probably had a delightful sense of humour which, later in life, after her heartbreaking experiences with her lovers and her husband, expressed itself in bitter irony.

During her youth two unusual events in the Wesley household made a deep impression on Emily — one occurred while she was in her teens, and the other when she was about twenty-four years of age.

The first was the rectory fire in 1709. The story of the fire had been repeated many times, and it has been made famous by the dramatic rescue from the flames of John or "Jacky," then a lad of about five. His mother believed he had been saved for a purpose, and she decided to give special attention to his spiritual development. The effect on Emily, however, was more indirect. After the fire, the members of the family were scattered for

Some signatures gathered by Adam Clarke and reproduced in the 1823 London edition of his MEMOIRS OF THE WESLEY FAMILY. Notice how closely the signature of Martha Wesley (number 8) resembles that of John Wesley (number 5) who taught her to write.

---

shelter among friends and relatives, but Emily remained with her parents. She drew very close to her mother and developed an affection for her that never wavered in spite of Susanna's ruthless decision much later to prevent Emily from marrying the man of her choice—her first and only true love. In addition, within a year of the fire, Emily suddenly realized the indebtedness that forever after hung over the rectory like a cloud. "I began to find out we were ruined!" she wrote to her brother, John, and she was right. (Stev, p. 263) The Wesleys never recovered financially from the effects of the fire. It cost about four hundred pounds to rebuild the rectory and the expense was so great the house was never more than half furnished. For about a dozen years also neither Mrs. Wesley nor her children had half enough clothing. To add to the expense of the situation, her father for several consecutive winters lived in London, probably as a delegate to Convocation, allowing his family to shift for themselves in intolerable want and affliction. ". . . then I learned," wrote Emily to John Wesley, "what it was to seek money for bread, seldom having any without such hardship in getting it that much abated the pleasure of it." (Stev, p. 263)

The other event in her life had to do with the poltergeist, the ghostly creature that haunted the Wesley household from December 1716 through

January 1717, and possibly until March or April. John Wesley, who was at Charterhouse School, London, during this time, later requested each member of the family to write an account of the rappings, groanings, levitations, and violence that frightened everyone except the doughty rector, himself. John eventually published the accounts in *The Arminian Magazine*. Emily's account, written at first for her brother, Samuel, is quite lengthy. Its importance lies in the fact that the hauntings convinced Emily of the reality of another world. She wrote:

> . . . I am so far from being superstitious that I was too much inclined to infidelity, so that I heartily rejoice at having such an opportunity of convincing myself, past doubt or scruple, of the existence of some beings besides those we see. (DW p. 24)

She was thoroughly convinced of the "reality of the thing" and attributed the weird manifestation to witchcraft. She was the only one of the Wesleys who reported hearing the ghost later in life — when she was well past middle age.

However, her usual sense of humor colored the experience, and it was she who laughed away fear by referring to the ghost as "Old Jeffrey," a name which was immediately adopted by the whole family, especially when it was remembered that an old man by that name had died in the rectory attic.

On the other hand, the ghost never whetted her interest in the occult as it did her brother, John. For the rest of his life John was excited by tales of the supernatural. Whenever he found an example, however irrational, he included it in his *Journal* or published it in *The Arminian Magazine*.

Two further events occurred which influenced Emily's life. Her brother, John, had written to his mother on November 1, 1724, saying, among other things:

> . . . I should be exceedingly glad to keep a correspondence with my sister Emily, if she were willing; for I believe I have not heard from her since I was at Oxford. (JWL, I, p. 151)

The challenge, which was passed on to Emily, resulted in a lifelong relationship and a constant correspondence between John and Emily, only a small portion of which survives. She and John became confidants, and she wrote to him of her inmost thoughts which she begged him never to reveal to a soul.

A turning point came in Emily's life when, fully realizing the hopeless poverty of her family, she decided to go up to London to seek work as a governess. She lived for a time with her father's brother — her Uncle Matthew Wesley. He was a wealthy, practicing physician, perhaps a surgeon, although in his will he refers to himself as an apothecary. He moved in an upper middle class circle, and he was always glad to welcome any of his nieces who came to visit him.

By now Emily was a woman of full maturity, well-shaped, and attractive in appearance. She was quick-witted, had a pleasing personality, and was sufficiently educated to enable her to take part brilliantly in social conversation. Her happiness and contentment may also have been born of a sense of security and even superiority—she was a Wesley!

London and Leybourne

Emily's Uncle Matthew was wealthy, exceedingly generous, and a sound, practical man of affairs. He tolerated his brother, Samuel, although, as a dissenter, he disliked his brother's rigid Anglicanism. He sympathized with his brother's wife, but he was never quite comfortable with his nephews, John and Charles. Eventually he came to respect the work they were doing, although in the beginning he had doubted their sincerity. He enjoyed the company of Emily whose cheerful, orderly, contented pattern of life fitted well into his manner of living.

It was at the home of her Uncle Matthew that Emily met the only man she ever truly loved. His name was Robert Leybourne. He had been educated at Westminster School, where he became acquainted with Emily's brother, Samuel, and in 1711, at seventeen years of age, had matriculated at Brasenose College. He matriculated at Christ Church in 1712. In 1717 he was elected a Fellow at Brasenose College and was awarded an M.A. degree. In 1723 to '24 he was a Junior Proctor. Later in life he had a successful career in the Anglican Church. Through his mother's brother he inherited considerable wealth.

Leybourne was a friend of John Wesley who seemed to think well of him. Emily probably first met him at the home of her uncle when he was a Fellow at Brasenose College. At any rate, he captivated the heart of Emily at once. From that day forward, and for many years after, there was no other man on the horizon of her life but Robert Leybourne.

This is not surprising. Until this time she had met and been courted by only the swains at Epworth or Wroot. Most of them were rough, crude fellows who lacked the education and the graces that shined forth so clearly in the life and manner of Robert Leybourne. We have no hint as to his physical appearance, but his dress and social suavity must have been impeccable. John Wesley once noted a quarrel between Samuel Wesley, Jr. and Leybourne in which the latter behaved with kindliness and dignity, going out of his way to heal the breach between them. John adds, "We were several times entertained by him, and, I thought, very handsomely . . .", (JWL, I, p. 168) no small compliment from a man of John Wesley's critical nature.

Emily was literally swept off her feet. For the first time she was madly, madly in love. Forgotten, for the moment, were the hardships and frustrations of Epworth. Forgotten was "Old Jeffrey" and the country lovers she may have secretly met when "Old Jeffrey" was quiet and there was no reason to search the grounds for an apparition. The affable Uncle Matthew saw no harm in the youth's visits, and did nothing to stop them.

The moment came when Leybourne whispered in Emily's ear the magic words, "I love you!" and Emily's world was complete. That this well-mannered, highly educated man with his impeccable manners, his social graces by which he could have commanded the love of many women, should love her, lifted Emily to a shattering ecstasy. He was everything she had ever dreamed for or wanted. She described him to her brother John as a person of "the highest understanding and . . . the sweetest temper in England. . . ." (Stev, p. 266)

Unfortunately, Emily was not able to find work in London and was forced to return home. However, life was still sweet. She corresponded regularly with Leybourne. For three years she nestled like a bird in its nest in the warmth of his affection. She expressed what Leybourne and his love meant to her in a letter to her brother John:

> . . . When anything grieved me he was my comforter; when affliction pressed hard on me he was at hand to relieve me; . . . although our affairs grew no better, yet I was tolerable easy, thinking his love sufficient recompense for the loss or absence of all other worldly comforts.

Then suddenly tragedy struck, like a crash of thunder on a clear summer day or a flash flood in a narrow canyon.

> . . . a near relation laid the groundwork of my misery, and, joined with my mother's command and my own indiscretion, broke the correspondence between him and I. (Stev, p. 263)

The near relative was probably her brother Samuel. Generally a well-balanced, well-poised clergyman, he, nevertheless, seems to have taken a dislike to Robert Leybourne. It is possible it was actually Samuel's wife who was not enamoured of the brilliant student and lover; or maybe Samuel remembered some youthful indiscretion in Leybourne's past. He might have doubted the man's sincerity. At any rate, he seems to have shared his concerns with his mother and convinced her of Leybourne's unfitness for marriage, especially for marriage with Emily. It was Susanna, herself, who gave a direct command to her daughter to break off her relationship with Leybourne. Emily states that there was some indiscretion of her own that was involved in the break-up.

It would help if we knew what were Samuel's objections to Leybourne, what was Emily's indiscretion, and why Susanna so adamantly set about breaking her daughter's heart. All we know is that the sweet, good-tempered, contented Emily experienced a slow change in her disposition and in her outlook on life. She wrote to John:

> That dismal winter I shall ever remember: my mother was sick, confined to her bed, my father in danger of arrests every day [for in-

debtedness]. I had a large family to keep, and a small sum to keep it on; expecting my mother's death every day, and my father's confinement; and yet in all this care, the loss of Leybourne was heaviest. For near half a year I never slept half a night, and, now, provoked at all my relations, resolved never to marry. (Stev, p. 263)

It is strange that Emily's father does not seem to have had anything to do with either the love affair or its dismal ending. He apparently was too busy with his scholarly pursuits or dodging a debtor's jail. It is strange also that Emily, who was as self-reliant and independent as any of the Wesleys, should have bowed so completely to her mother's will; especially since she must have known her mother was influenced by her son, Samuel, Jr.

It may be, of course, that Emily herself, was beginning to doubt Leybourne's sincerity. Sometime later she said as much to John. Three years is a long time to court someone by correspondence alone, and one wonders why Leybourne, after he learned of Mrs. Wesley's attitude toward him, did not drop everything in London and ride to Epworth forthwith and claim the one he professed to love. Maybe Emily's sleeplessness was caused not so much by her mother's command as by Leybourne's readiness to give up without a fight. Emily loved the man with the intense passion of a woman who has never before deeply loved anyone; but he failed her. She was passionate, he was polite. When he learned that Emily's parents disapproved of him, he calmly dropped her.

Four years later Emily is still in love with Leybourne. She asks her brother John not to withdraw his friendship from Leybourne, but to assist him in his distress.

Leybourne's "distress," whatever it was, must have been very minor. Probably Emily thought that through John's friendship with her former lover she might gain his attention. She was happy to have any news of Leybourne, and on one occasion wrote to John thanking him for inquiring after Leybourne. "He shifts place so quick," she added, "that 'tis hard to find him but not impossible." (Stev, p. 266)

Leybourne eventually received a good living in the Anglican church, inherited money from his family, was twice married, both times happily.

The whole troubled incident changed Emily's disposition from that of a sweet, contented person, to one soured by life and increasingly critical of her fellow human beings. When, as we shall see, her sister, Hetty, eloped to London against her parents' wishes, returning the next day unmarried and disillusioned, Emily and possibly her mother were among the last of the family to forgive her. (See Chapter Five)

Eventually Emily became convinced that whatever stories had been circulated about Leybourne were insitgated by pure malice, possibly by either

her brother Samuel or his wife. It is difficult to say. She was sure, however, that Leybourne was a good man. She does not say who she believed had maligned him or why.

A New Beginning

Previous to this discovery, Emily had learned of a vacancy in a boarding school at Lincoln. Applying for the position, she was accepted, and remained here for five years. Here she was as happy as she ever would be. She enjoyed teaching and, as she wrote to John, "fell readily into that way of life." (Stev, p. 263)

For the first time she had her own money, was able to purchase some good clothes, had money left over for small luxuries, and received the respect due her position and her ability. The search for love was temporarily dismissed as she fulfilled a strong craving for a career. Unfortunately, the school broke up, as she states it. This was not necessarily a tragedy, for with her five years' experience she might easily have secured another position. But now her parents pressured her to come home. Her mother was especially desirous for her return. She may have wanted Emily's practical help in running the household. She may have, by now, regretted her interference in Emily's affair with Leybourne. She certainly painted a picture of life at Epworth far different from what Emily had experienced. There was evidently more sociability with friends in the parish and friends at Bawtry and Doncaster, and other places. Emily, herself, Susanna promised, would be allowed greater liberties. Furthermore, Mr. Wesley's prospects were improving. He had received, in addition to the living at Epworth, the parish at Wroot. If things continued as everyone hoped they would, the Wesleys soon would be rich.

"In an evil hour" (Stev, p. 263) as she expressed it, Emily allowed herself to be persuaded and returned home. She found things changing in her family, but not economically. Her sister Susanna was married (see Chapter Three), Anne was soon to be married (see Chapter Six), Hetty was in her living hell caused by her unsuccessful affair (see Chapter Five), and Martha was centering her life in London. Emily's greatest disappointment was in her father's inability to manage his financial affairs. The expected wealth never materialized. When Emily had used up her savings and had to turn to her parents for assistance, she learned the true situation. Her father was hopelessly in debt, partly because of mismanagement of his income, partly because of his readiness to assist his sons at Oxford, partly because of his liberality to those outside his family, and partly because of his expensive trips to London. Emily, in writing to John, boldly states what she had probably expressed at home:

> I know not when we had so good a year, both at Wroote and at Epworth, as this year; but instead of saving anything to clothe my sister or myself, we are just where we were. A noble crop has almost all gone, beside Epworth living, to pay some part of those infinite debts my father has

run into, which are so many, as I have lately found out, that were he to save fifty pounds a year he would not be clear in the world this seven years. So here is a fine prospect indeed of his growing rich!

Emily still had a tremendous affection for her mother:

> While my mother lives I am inclined to stay with her; she is so very good to me, [because of the guilt she may have felt after forcing Emily and Leybourne apart?] and has so little comfort in the world besides, that I think it barbarous to abandon her. . . . Whatever people may say of me here, I hope to meet with happiness in the other world if not in this; (Stev, p. 264)

There is little doubt that the home of the Wesleys was not the idyllic haven some biographers and churchmen have attempted to picture. In the end, the critical state of affairs which she faced began to undermine Emily's health, and she looked for some means of escape from family problems.

New Prospects and a New Lover

About 1727 Emily accepted a position as a teacher in the boarding school of a Mrs. Taylor in Lincoln. Probably her previous experience as a teacher in Lincoln opened the way to this new position which, unfortunately, did not prove to be a happy one.

Emily carried heavy responsibilities at the school. In addition, Mrs. Taylor was a hard taskmaster and allegedly a bad employer, doing everything possible to delay or even avoid paying Emily her salary regularly. Kezzy, Emily's youngest sister, was recruited for a time both as a student and to assist in the school, but Mrs. Taylor evidently made life impossible, and Emily eventually considered resigning. She finally made her decision following a brief stay at Epworth, where she went to care for her sister, Susanna, who was seriously ill. Evidently, Emily's mother relied on her greatly and was constantly seeking her help.

When Emily returned to Lincoln she resigned her position to found her own school at Gainsborough. In 1731 she entered upon this new venture enthusiastically and full of hope for the future. She wrote to John:

> I have a fairer prospect at Gainsborough even than I could hope for; my greatest difficulty will be want of money at my first entrance. I shall furnish my school with canvas, worsteds, silks etc. etc., and am much afraid of being dipped in debt at the first; but God's will be done! Troubles of that kind are what I have been used to. Will you lend me the other three pounds, which you designed for me at Lady Day? It would help me much. You will if you can, I am sure, for so would I do by you, . . . I am knitting brother Charles a fine purse; give my love to him, - I am dear brother, your loving sister and constant friend. (Stev. p. 268)

She probably received the three pounds she requested and further aid from Samuel Wesley, Jr. and a great deal of assistance from her Uncle Matthew. From the beginning the school proved a success.

Emily was about forty years of age now, when she could hardly have expected the advent of another lover. However, she was an attractive woman, and this time she was courted by a medical gentleman — maybe a physician. He lived in the neighborhood and, for a time, Emily may have been his housekeeper. She also continued her work at the school. He soon became a delightful companion, a faithful friend, and eventually a passionate lover.

Once again her family interfered. This time John sought to break up the romance. His only objection to the man was his religion — he was a Quaker.

Emily was both shocked and grieved. Again, it was a question of her lover or her family — John or the Quaker. Unfortunately, at about the time John was strongly stating his objections to the affair, Emily and her Quaker friend had a violent quarrel. Both were opinionated persons — he a Whig, she a Tory. In addition, he was exceedingly jealous. Emily described the quarrel in a letter to John. She first states that she was uncertain what to do about continuing the friendship. She weighed her decision carefully. One week she would be in pleasant conversation with him, the next week she would refuse to see him. She wanted to please both her lover and John. Finally, the quarrel occurred that tipped the scales in John's favor. She gives a vivid description of the quarrel:

> . . . You must understand his Whiggish principles were always more provoking to me than his being a Quaker. One morning I chanced to say at breakfast that my father was gone to Oxford. Immediately he fell foul on that University, and complimented them with several titles which I thought their enemies had more right to. We then got to Lord Clarendon and the family of the Stuarts, he decrying them, and I, with more warmth, vindicating them.
>
> The dispute lasted hot about two hours, and we parted with mutual resentment, I believe; at least I was thoroughly provoked at him for daring to contradict me so violently, it being, you know, my avowed doctrine that an unmarried woman can never be in the wrong in any conversation with a bachelor. Well, this provoked me, and soon after his back was up ten times worse than mine — the occasion as follows. We have here, boarding with me, one Robinson, a young saddler from London, who seems to like home better than being abroad. As the doctor is naturally the most suspicious fool breathing, he seldom comes into the house without first watching the window; and I fancy one evening he saw him leaning on my chair and talking to me, for the next morning he began a long grave harangue on the inconstancy of womankind, and, what was worse, he affirmed that our sex was so fond of vanity, that no woman could or would be contented with the address and company of one man. I perceived where the shoe pinched, and answered as gravely that no man had reason to complain of a woman keeping another company except he himself had plainly offered her marriage and she had entertained him afterwards; and added that none but a fool would complain of being jilted by a woman never courted in express terms. So, scorning to vindicate my conduct, I left him to his meditations, and never have been with him in private and very little in public since, nor do I

design to ever show the least regard more above common civility. So farewell George Fox, and all thy tribe, for Rockwood, and Ringwood, and Howler and Tray! (Stev, p. 269)

And so because of a foolish quarrel, she dismissed her lover! Later in the same letter she makes it quite plain that the quarrel was only an excuse for bringing the affair to an end. She had felt the grief of her brother's displeasure more than the joy she might have found in her lover's presence. But, in spite of her light-hearted attitude toward the break with her Quaker lover, she felt the loss of his company as keenly as a person feels the slash of a sharp knife. Toward the end of her letter she expresses the bitterness she felt at this disappointing turn of events:

. . . but now what is there left in life worth valuing? Truly not much, and if I should comply with my mother's earnest desire — throw up my business here and go home — I do not see there would be much in it, since my Creator seems to have decreed me to a state of suffering here, and always deprives me of what I love, or embitters it to me. Who can contend with Omnipotence? (Stev, p. 270)

Sometime after this, Emily's father died. She had never been very close to him, except as a child. In fact, once when he visited her at Lincoln she wrote to John:

. . . I presume you want to be informed concerning my father's affairs at Epworth. He was here before Christmas, little to my satisfaction by the way; he seemed very reserved to me, and I the same to him. (Stev. p. 266)

Her affection for her mother continued to know no bounds. When her mother became a widow she lived for a time with Emily at Gainsborough. John, however, could not help but notice the gradual change in the tone of Emily's letters, and in a rather stern note he expressed his concern for her spiritual welfare. She replied to him in a lengthy letter defending her religious sincerity and challenging his. The letter is filled with good sense, sound philosophy and logical reasoning. She also strikes at Wesley's purported holiness, pointing out that his constant preoccupation with God and religion may be due to his having lost his dear Mrs. C.____ who, in spite of Wesley's expressed interest in her, had married a school teacher. "and now," adds Emily, "the mind which is an active principle, losing its aim here, has fixed on its Maker for happiness." (Stev, p. 272)

Mrs. C____ was Sally Kirkham, with whom Wesley might well have been in love before she married someone else. At any rate, Emily's analysis is like a shot across the bow and must have caused Wesley to think. Before she finishes this brilliant letter Emily assures here brother of her love and states that whatever faults she has been guilty of with respect to God, to Wesley she has been blameless, "except loving you too well has been one" [a fault].

Emily Becomes Mrs. Harper

Emily Wesley finally became married sometime in the Year 1735. She was married by her brother to a Robert Harper, an apothecary, shortly before John left England in October of that year as a missionary to the Indians in Georgia. The Harpers were a well-known family in Epworth, but Emily seems to have confided to no one that she was being courted and was seriously considering marriage. Probably she had learned that she would need to trust her own judgment exclusively if she were to be married at all. Unfortunately, her judgment in this case was poor.

The marriage could have been a happy one. The position of an apothecary in the eighteenth century, although not as lucrative as that of a physician, was one of importance in the community and generally afforded a good living to a person of reasonable ability and good business sense.

Only the wealthy could afford a physician in the eighteenth century. The lower middle class and the poor visited the apothecary who listened carefully to the description of their complaints. He then visited a physician who, for a fee, suggested a remedy. The apothecary then sold the medicine to the patient. The practice, however, required that the apothecary have a shop where he kept his drugs and medicines and that he be on a cordial relationship with a physician. Apparently Robert Harper lacked both of these requirements. He seems to have traveled from place to place and pursued his trade in a more or less unorthodox fashion.

He was more than eager, however, to marry Emily Wesley. How he captured her fancy is a mystery. He must have had some redeeming qualities, but no one seems to know what they were. After the wedding, the couple lived at Gainsborough where Emily continued with her school. Harper had no scruples in helping himself to the profits from her work but contributed little to the expenses of the household. As a lover he was a mistake, as a husband and provider he was a disaster. They soon were in deep poverty. They had one daughter who probably died in infancy, although she may have lived for several years since she is mentioned in the will of Emily's Uncle Matthew, who bequeathed her one hundred pounds. In all probability Harper, himself, died about 1740 when Emily left Gainsborough and came to London. One authority believed Harper absconded with her small savings, leaving her destitute. It is impossible to say. If Harper died it is hardly likely that Emily mourned his death. By this time Emily was a sharp-tongued woman who had borne more than her share of life's adversities. A letter written to her brother John in November 1738, sometime before her husband's probable death, explains her problems and reveals her state of mind. To understand it we must understand the circumstances that prompted Emily to write as she did.

When John Wesley returned to London from Georgia in 1738, he passed through what many biographers considered a spiritual watershed experience at a Moravian prayer meeting in Aldersgate Street. Some refer to this experience as his conversion. Others see in it merely another step in his religious development. The experience, however, had been under the guidance of the Moravians which led him to journey to Herrnhut, Germany in order to study at its source the Moravian view of faith. He departed from England without visiting Emily at Gainsborough and without providing any financial help for either his sisters or his mother. Samuel, Jr. and Charles did what they could for their mother and Emily. Emily was deeply hurt by John's seeming indifference. The situation was made considerably worse when, on John's return from Germany, he wrote Emily a letter concerning, not her problems, but concerning the spiritual state of the church in Germany. It never entered his mind that Emily might be so harrassed by the need for making ends meet and by her concern for her mother, who was now living elsewhere, that she would not have the slightest interest in the churches of Germany.

When Emily received John's letter she wrote a biting reply. Earlier in their correspondence she would probably have written in a lighter vein. Her letter might have been filled with humorous touches and she might have gently pointed out how his indifference to her needs had deeply hurt her. Now she wrote:

> Dear Brother, — Yours I received, and thank you for remembering me, though your letter afforded me small consolation. For God's sake, tell me how a distressed woman, who expects daily to have the very bed taken from under her for rent, can consider the state of the Churches in Germany. I am ready to give up the ghost with grief; how is it possible in such extremity to think of anybody's concerns but my own, till this storm is blown over some way, or my head laid low in Gainsborough Churchyard? We owe at Christmas two years rent for this house; and as it was my hard hap to marry a tradesman without a trade, the burden of the day has lain upon me from the beginning, . . . I have sold many of my clothes for bread — is not that calamity? I want many of the common necessaries of life; I am almost always sick, . . . I have yet a bed to lie on, but Christmas will soon be here, and if Bob Harper will do nothing to raise half a years rent I cannot get it myself, though I am somewhat towards it; but 'tis a cold time of year to be turned out of doors. Sam and Charles, God bless them, kept me safe at midsummer.

Her letter continues to outline her problems and difficulties, and she finally ends the missive by explaining what hurt her most in John's conduct:

> . . . Had you the same, nay a quarter of the love to me I have for you, long since you would have been with me; it was in your power — you, who could go to Germany, could you not reach Gainsborough? Yes certainly; and had my soul been lost by self murder, my damnation would have justly laid at your door. (Stev, p. 273)

We do not know how this letter affected John Wesley. There is no record of an immediate reply. However, in 1743 he wrote her a caustic letter, indeed.

Emily had in 1740 moved to London where John Wesley had built a chapel on the ruins of a plant once used for casting cannon and popularly known as The Foundery. In addition, he had erected a house for lay preachers, a coach-house and stable and an apartment for his own use. His mother came here in 1739, and Emily and her favorite maid took up quarters here in 1740. Here also the surviving sisters of John Wesley often met with their mother until her death in 1742. Emily and her maid continued for a time living in Wesley's apartment and at Wesley's expense. Emily evidently wrote a number of complaining letters to her brother, probably one too many. He answered her letter from Newcastle, calling her "Emmy."

By this time Emily seems to have become thoroughly embittered with her lot. The once contented Emily, who read a pleasant book after her day's work at Epworth parsonage, had become the shrewish "Emmy" with a sharp tongue. Although some might condemn her for this change, most people will be able to understand it.

However, in his letter, John is downright cruel to her. In John's defense, we should remember that he hated complaints. He once said that when a person complained to him it was like tearing the flesh from his bones. And evidently Emily complained frequently. He ended his letter by writing:

> You are of all creatures the most unthankful to God and man. I stand amazed at you. How little have you profited under such means of improvement! Surely, whenever your eyes are opened, whenever you see your own tempers, with the advantages you have enjoyed, you will make no scruple to pronounce yourself (whores and murderers not excepted) the very chief of sinners. I am etc. (JWL, II, p. 100)

The letter may indeed seem harsh (and at this distance in time a little amusing), but we must remember John was supplying food and lodging for both his sister and her favorite maid, besides carrying the financial and spiritual burdens and responsibilities of the Methodist Societies that he was establishing throughout England. It is amazing that he did not lose his temper more often.

Emily — The Methodist

John and Emily, however, had too deep a respect for each other to allow these exchanges to make a real breach in their affections. Some of Emily's later letters are written in the same spirit of love and understanding that was so much a part of her former correspondence. Emily eventually became a Methodist.

Her appreciation of Methodism, however, was not the result of sudden decision. As early as August 4, 1740 she had written a letter to her brother questioning many of the doctrines and practices of his movement. "The Methodists make a mighty noise in the nation," she wrote, "Most people condemn their doctrines, yet whether out of curiosity or goodness I cannot tell. Never were any preachers more followed. Mr. Rogers and Mr. Ingham at Nottingham preached lately to upward of ten thousand souls."

She then asked her brother "to solve her a few scruples." She questions the doctrine of faith as held by the Methodist. She wonders why faith is necessary to a state of salvation, and if so, to what purpose is infant baptism? Or what becomes of those who died before they come to an age capable of believing? She thrusts hard at the idea of Christian perfection and states that there is none who has arrived at absolute perfection.

She criticizes the Methodists for preaching in the fields and in the markets, and wonders what becomes of "our excellent liturgy which cannot be used in such places." She cannot understand why the Methodists condemn some of the world's finest literature. She ends by stating, ". . . if God have raised you up to reform the nation, I heartily wish you prosperity. I believe all the Methodists to be good Christians, though not infallible. May the Spirit of truth (who alone is so) guide us into all truth, . . ." (JLW, II, p. 23)

On June 17th, 1741 she wrote him another letter about his beliefs and practices which she thought were absorbing too much of his time and affection.

> . . . Your zeal for God's glory ought not to eat up natural affection. If I be not perfect as the Methodists I am a firm member of the Church of England, and endeavor to practice my known duty; and as all our doings without charity are nothing worth, you ought not to judge me for not holding all you believe. I am glad at heart you oppose Whitefield in his horrid doctrines of predestination, and wish your were as free from the Romish errors of auricular confession and bodily austerities on one hand, and the Quaker fancies of absolute perfection etc., on the other; but above all that you would not imitate those deluded people the French Prophets, in casting out devils — except you would be so good to cast the devil of poverty out of my pocket, a place he frequently haunts. . . . (JLW, II, p. 63)

She then points out that he has sufficient funds at his command to assist in making her more comfortable than formerly but wonders if "Maybe the Methodists confine all charity to their own sect."

Her attitude towards Methodism, however, was going through a decided change. Possibly her mother, who strongly supported John and his movement, had influenced Emily's thought. As we noted, Emily was at the Foundery when her mother died. She was at her bedside with her sisters when her mother said quietly, "My children, when I am released, sing a psalm of praise!" And with Emily, they did.

It has been said that no one achieves peace in later life who has not first settled the problem of religious faith. Certainly Emily Wesley, as she grew older, listened more and more carefully to the teachings of her brother John. We do not know when or where or how she became a Methodist, but she did find a faith similar to his. Maybe this caused the final change in her personality.

For about the last twenty-five years of her life she lived in rooms at the Methodist Chapel in West Street, London. Here she performed the work of a deaconess. She visited the sick, the needy, the poor. She entered their homes constantly, and she was greatly loved by the Methodists. She was especially kind to those in need and to the suffering. She knew the meaning of personal tragedy and utter despair. For a time her sister Martha came to live with her.

We do not know how much correspondence passed between her and John during these years, but by 1750 their relationship is so close that John informed her that he is to marry Mrs. Vazeille and would like to bring her to meet Emily. She accepted the news gracefully, but refused to meet Wesley's wife on the ground that "Alas, I am to weak, too low in the world for you to bring a new wife to see. This is not Lincoln or Gainsbro'. At either of these places matters would have been different." (JWL, II, p. 449)

John respected Emily's wishes, although, he, himself, often visited her at West Street, and both brother and sister enjoyed their continuing relationship.

Her lodgings were so near the main meeting house that, by throwing open a window, she could hear the services after she was confined to her bed by her recurring illness. She died in 1771, at the beginning of her eightieth year. Her search for love had finally ended. She had loved her mother who, in some ways, had failed her; she had loved Robert Leybourne who was driven from her by her family, she had loved Harper who was unworthy of her; she had loved her brother John who often disappointed her, and now − ? She was probably centering her love in God.

A strange circumstance occurred while she was at West Street. In a letter to her brother John she mentions that "Old Jeffrey" the ghost of Epworth, had visited her on several occasions. She first mentions the apparition in a letter written in 1750 (JWL, II, p. 449), the year all of London was concerned and shocked by an earthquake that destroyed a considerable amount of property and killed a large number of people. Some were sure the judgment day had come. In the midst of the excitement "Old Jeffrey" again rapped his greeting to Emily, although she does not seem too sure about the whole incident. Maybe the signal was only in her imagination! Maybe she sought assurance once again of the existence of that other and possibly better world−a world in which she would find the love for which she had sought and which she had faith to believe must reign supreme.

Chapter Three

A Case of Wife Abuse
The Story of Susanna Wesley
Mrs. Richard Ellison

Childhood and Youth

Susanna Wesley, usually called "Sukey," second oldest of the seven sisters in search of love, was born about 1695 at South Ormsby. There is no extant record of her baptism; but this is not surprising since records were often lost through fires or plain carelessness. She was the third surviving child of her parents, Samuel Wesley, Sr. and Susanna. By the time she was born her mother had given birth to five other children.

She matured into a good-natured, happy, vivacious girl who loved life and had a delightful sense of humor. She was self-willed but not opinionated. Once she made up her mind, she was not easily moved. Although she possessed an out-going personality, she was an exceedingly private person. She kept her own counsel. Unlike her sister, Emily, she had no confidant among her brothers and sisters to whom she revealed her innermost thoughts. Doubtless the young farmers of Epworth and Wroot clustered about her. She was fun to be with, and she brought laughter as the sun brings warmth.

Authorities differ as to her mental endowments. George T. Stevenson, in his *Memorials of The Wesley Family,* notes that she wrote few letters and that these do not convey any degree of high culture and intelligence (Stev, p. 279). They center in the stories of "Old Jeffrey," the ghost, and they were written only after considerable prodding by her brother Samuel, Jr. Other authorities believe that she was highly intelligent and that her refusal to write letters, even to her brother, John, who in 1724 noted that he had written to her twice without eliciting a reply, came more from lack of interest than any lack of talent. Indeed she must have had a thoughtful and serious side. It was to her that her mother wrote a long epistle setting forth her most profound thoughts on religion, concluding with a keen analysis of the Apostles' Creed. Her mother evidently believed that her daughter, Susanna, was not only capable of understanding the letter but also would enjoy reading it.

Susanna had the advantage not only of receiving the early schooling provided for each of the Wesleys by their parents, but also of living for a time with her Uncle Matthew in London. Her sojourn in London came about, the first time, through the disastrous fire that destroyed the Epworth rectory in 1709. After the fire, the Wesley children, with the exception of Emily, were placed with relatives and friends. Susanna and her younger sister, Mehetabel, went to London to live with their father's brother, Uncle Matthew.

30

By 1716 Susanna was in Epworth once again, where she witnessed the antics of the rectory ghost. In describing "Old Jeffrey's" conduct to her brother, Samuel, she emphasized the humourous aspects of the story more than did her sisters or her parents. She was loath to write at all, since she evidently cared little about letter-writing. She apparently expected her father or sisters to give Samuel a full account of the events. She insisted that Samuel tell no one she had written to him. Maybe she was recalling that she seldom answered letters and she did not want to offend anyone to whom she had not written. Her account, however, is delightful reading. It is she who, possibly with a chuckle, states:

> It [Old Jeffrey] is now pretty quiet, only at our repeating prayers for the king and prince, when it usually begins, [knocking] especially when my father says "Our most gracious Sovereign Lord," etc. This my father is angry at, and designs to say *three* instead of *two* [prayers] for the royal family. (DW, p. 21)

In the next letter to Samuel she writes of another amusing incident:

> . . . One thing I believe you do not know—that is, last Sunday, to my father's no small amazement, his trencher danced upon the table a pretty while, without anybody's stirring the table. When lo! an adventurous wretch took it up, and spoiled the sport, for it remained still ever after. (DW, p. 27)

Susanna enjoyed "Old Jeffrey" more than any other of the Wesleys.

Uncle Annesley

After these events Susanna lived for a time in London with her Uncle Annesley, her mother's brother. Annesley was a strange, mysterious character. He apparently was a man of considerable wealth, or, at least, he gave that impression. He journeyed to India where he was factor of the East India Company in Surat. He was out of touch with his family until one day he supposedly wrote a letter to his sister, Mrs. Wesley, stating that he was returning to London from India. He invited her to meet him in London, promising her a sizeable gift of money. Mrs. Wesley went to London, waited for the ship, but Annesley was not on board. He was never heard from again. What mystery lies behind his disappearance no one knows.

Dr. Frank Baker, a prominent Wesleyan scholar, presents a slightly different version of the tale. In a footnote to a letter written by John Wesley to his brother, Samuel—in which John mentions his Uncle Annesley—Dr. Baker writes:

> Mrs. Wesley's brother, Samuel Annesley (c. 1658-1732), factor of the East India Company in Surat, India, whose return in one of the company's ships had been reported in the press, so that she came down to London to meet him, only to be confronted by his mysterious disappearance. John Wesley passed on to his own nephews the tradition of

a missing fortune promised by this rich uncle to the Epworth Wesleys, in spite of a tiff between him and Samuel Wesley, Sr., but the tradition was exploded this century by the discovery of his will, cutting them each off with a shilling. (JWL, I, P. 146)

Annesley obviously was an eccentric. He may have indeed promised Mrs. Wesley a sum of money, possibly regretting what he had written in his will. However, if he wrote to Mrs. Wesley, it must have been from India, and his will was in London. There would be difficulties in changing it. There is no explaining his conduct.

However, he was especially pleased with his niece, Susanna, who lived at his home before his sojourn in India. He apparently approved of her manners, her open disposition, her affectionate nature and her lively intelligent personality. Before he left for India he promised her a handsome present which seems to have greatly excited Susanna's hopes. However, to her great disappointment, the gift never materialized.

Marriage and "Dick" Ellison

About the year 1719 Susanna married Richard Ellison, a wealthy landowner whom she must have known in her childhood and whom she met again at her Uncle Matthew's home. The date of the marriage is not certain and there are no extant records to confirm it. Mrs. Wesley believed that Susanna rashly threw herself upon the man, partly because of his wealth and partly in pique because the gift promised by her Uncle Annesley had not been forthcoming. Certainly in marrying Ellison, Susanna acted without the permission or advice of her parents. Having known the Ellison family themselves, they could have warned her against what proved to be a very unfortunate match.

However, Susanna may not have listened to them. She had experienced the meaning of poverty in her parents' home, and she understood something of its devastating effects. She may, therefore, have been captured by the fact that Ellison was a gentleman farmer and a wealthy property owner whom she believed she loved. He, himself, on the other hand, may have assumed the initiative, mistaking Susanna's open, friendly, out-going personality and manner as an indication of her affection for him. Doubtless Susanna honestly thought she was marrying a gentleman farmer of good prospects and considerable wealth. Of a naturally affectionate nature, she must have thought that in Ellison she had found someone to love and someone who loved her. His wealth, while not necessary to her happiness, was certainly no handicap to their relationship.

Instead of being a gentleman, Ellison proved to be a coarse, vulgar, immoral man. At least that is what Mrs. Wesley said of him. She also said that Ellison was a little inferior to the apostate angels, a plague to Susanna and an afflication to the family. Samuel Wesley, Sr. stated that "Dick" Ellison was the "wen" of his family, whose company at the rectory was less pleasant to him than all his physic.

It is difficult to say in exactly what ways Ellison abused his wife. Susanna was not a letter-writer, as we have noted, and, in spite of her out-going personality, she was a very private person. She did not talk much about her marital problems. One biographer of the Wesleys, George J. Stevenson, wrote, "His conduct to his wife is represented as harsh, coarse and despotic, and under his unkindness, 'she well-night sank into the grave'" (Stev, p. 282). The love for which she sought had been fleeting.

The deterioration in their relationship can be noted more from the comments contained in the letters of Susanna's sisters and parents than in anything that Susanna, herself, reported.

In 1725, for example, Martha, in the course of a long letter to her brother, John, wrote, "Yet where a man has neither religion, birth, riches nor good nature, I can't see what a woman can expect but misery. My brother Ellison [Susanna's husband] wants all but riches . . ." (Stev, p. 360).

Two years later Samuel, Jr., in writing to John, stated in exasperation, "I wonder at nothing in relation to Dick [Ellison], who, if I mistake him not, does not desire to have it thought he has any religion, good nature or good manners." (Stev, p. 282)

Kezzy Wesley in writing to John in January 1729 says, "There has nothing happened since you left Lincoln that has had much effect upon my mind, except Dick [Ellison's] quarrel with his wife. There is no need of giving you a particular account of it." (Stev, p. 282)

In 1730 Martha in a letter to John revealed the deadly physical abuse her sister, Susanna, received at the hands of her husband:

> Dick is (if possible) 'tenfold more the child of Hell' than he used to be. He took it into his head 'tother night almost to beat out his wife's brains for taking his man off of him that was going to murder him — at least that made him cry out he had killed him. (JWL, I, P. 243)

Apparently the relationship had steadily deteriorated until in a drunken fit Ellison began physically abusing his wife. It would seem from Martha's account that Ellison was as cruel to his servants as to his wife. One of them openly rebelled and pounced upon Ellison, who began screaming that he was being murdered. At this juncture Susanna rushed to her husband's aid, only to have him turn upon her with a vicious attack in which he almost beat out her brains.

The amazing fact is that Ellison's treatment never broke her spirit, although it gradually changed her attitude toward him.

In 1731 the Ellisons came to Epworth for a visit and Kezzy wrote to John, "Sister Ellison is coming to live at Epworth again at Lady Day, which I am very sorry for; they will be a constant uneasiness to us." (Stev, p. 283) Later

Kezzy wrote again to John saying, "You may be sure he that increaseth knowledge of them increaseth sorrow." (Stev, p. 283) At one time Susanna's health broke under her husband's abuse, and it was thought she might die of consumption.

Susanna, nevertheless, tried her best to save the marriage. The couple had four children: John, Ann, Deborah, and Richard Annesley, one of whom at its birth almost cost Susanna her life. She sent for her mother, who found her as near death as anyone could be in life. Mrs. Wesley had come to her through a severe snowstorm and as a result contracted a serious cold and pleurisy. The situation was desperate. Emily came from Lincoln, where she was teaching in Mrs. Taylor's school, to assist for a time. Eventually the crisis passed. Susanna and her husband went on living much as before. Nothing changed in their marital life.

The marriage relationship eventually became so critical that when John Wesley and his party left England to serve as missionaries to the Indians in Georgia, he considered taking Susanna and possibly some of her children with him. The plan was abandoned. Samuel, Jr. wrote to John in Georgia:

> I don't blame you, upon the whole, for not taking my sister Ellison along with you, but I should have commended you exceedingly had you taken three or four of her children, who in all human probability in a few years may want conversion as much even as those poor people you are going among. (JWL, I, 460)

Apparently at the time Samuel had more concern for the Ellisons than John. However, his fears for the children were needless. George J. Stevenson, a Wesley biographer, took the trouble in 1876 to trace the children and grandchildren of Susanna and found that they turned out well, several becoming Methodists (Stev, p. 284 ff).

Up to this point Ellison was still a wealthy man. Although wealth does not necessarily bring happiness, it makes misfortune a little easier to bear. However, Ellison's personal fortune gradually declined. A disastrous fire destroyed his house and home and all the family's personal property. The members of the household scattered to take shelter among friends and relatives in London. Susanna, herself, left Ellison, never again to return to him. She did not explain why.

Was she frightened? Had the fire been caused by Ellison, himself, when in a drunken fury? Did his anger extend to further physical violence of which Susanna said nothing? Or was she simply tired of loving and seeking love from a man who so thoroughly disappointed her by his immorality, drunkeness, unkindness, physical abuse and unpredictability that she wanted nothing more to do with him? Who can tell? She never explained.

However, no sooner did Ellison realize that she was gone for good than he desperately wanted her back. That is understandable. Like all the Wesleys,

Susanna was good-looking, attractive, affectionate and kind-hearted. In addition, she was fun to be with. It is doubtful if the problems of her marriage altered her personality as Emily's problems had changed hers. In fact, Ellison understood his wife's spirit so well that he tried to take advantage of her affectionate nature by a deceptive trick to win her back. He advertised his own death! When Susanna heard of his decease she immediately returned to Lincoln to pay her last respects to her husband. To her amazement and surprise she found him very much alive and well. Possibly Ellison suspected she would be so relieved that she would put her arms around him and take him once more to her heart. She had no such intention. Once she understood the true situation she turned on her heel and disappeared into London. Here she literally hid herself among her family and friends.

Unfortunately, many women who have been abused by their husbands return to them again and again. Sometimes they return because they honestly love their spouses; other times because they have nowhere else to go. They desperately need the financial assistance their husbands can provide.

In Susanna's case, it is clear she no longer loved Richard Ellison. She had certainly married before she had clearly thought through whether or not her feeling for Ellison was truly love. Maybe the poverty in which she was reared caused her to attach too great an importance to Ellison's wealth. She gave the marriage a fair chance and the best she had. She was certainly searching for love and readily gave her love. But she must have known within a few months after the marriage that Ellison was a drunkard, a boor, and an immoral man. Nevertheless, she stayed with him and bore him four children. The time came, however, when she had had enough; and when she finally made up her mind, nothing or no one could change her. She was through with Dick Ellison.

In addition, Susanna was fortunate in that her brothers came to her rescue, particularly John. She was not dependent on Ellison for support. She was free of financial worries.

As for Ellison, greater misfortunes came upon him. All his land was under water for two years because of the failure of the Commissioners of Sewers to keep the drains open. Today the courts would have provided him relief and possibly adequate compensation. Ellison received nothing. He was completely ruined.

In his extremity he went to London and appealed to John Wesley, Susanna's brother. Wesley was never one to turn his back upon a pietous appeal. He looked upon Ellison not as a person who had injured his sister, but simply as a person in need — desperate need. Wesley turned to his wealthy banker friend, Ebenezer Blackwell, and arranged to have Ellison's name placed on a charity list in order to save him from a life in the gutter. Wesley wrote:

> You were so kind as to say (if I did not misunderstand you) that you
> had placed the name of Richard Ellison among those who were to have

a share of the money disposed of by Mr. Butterfield. Last night he called upon me. I find, all his cows are dead, and all his horses but one. And all his meadow land has been under water these two years (which is occasioned by the neglect of the Commissioners of the Sewers who ought to keep the drains open), so that he has very little to subsist on. Therefore, the smallest relief could never be more seasonable than at this time. (JWL, II, p. 493)

This kindness appeared to have reached the heart of Ellison, who became a Methodist. He may have thought, at first, that this step would link him once again with his wife. It did not. They may have encountered each other in some Methodist Class Meetings, for Susanna was now a Methodist also; but she wanted nothing more to do with her husband. Nevertheless, Ellison continued as a Methodist and died as a Methodist.

Charles Wesley in a letter dated April 11, 1760, wrote to his wife:

Yesterday evening I buried my brother Ellison. Sister Macdonald, whom he was always very fond of, prayed by him in his last moments. He told her he was not afraid to die, and believed God, for Christ's sake, had forgiven him. I felt a most solemn awe while I committed his body to the earth. (Stev., p. 284)

Not much is known of the remaining years of Susanna herself. She lived peacefully among her four children. They loved her and did everything in their power to make her life a happy one. Susanna had failed in her search for love in her marriage, but she found true love through her children. She lived mostly with her daughter Ann. Ann married twice. She first married a French Protestant refugee and, after his death, a gentleman named Gaunt. Ann Gaunt has been described as a fine looking, stout woman, under middle size, with an abundance of wit. In that respect she took after her mother. It was in her daughter's house that Susanna died.

Her nickname was "Sukey." John, in writing of her death to his brother Charles in 1764, states:

Sister Sukey was in huge agonies for five days, and then died in full assurance of faith. Some of her last words (after she had been speechless for some time) were, "Jesus is come! Heaven is here!" (JWLT, IV, p. 277)

Her quest was ended.

Chapter Four

Joy and Tragedy
The Story of Mary Wesley
Mrs. John Whitelamb

Childhood and Youth

It seems like an anomaly to link the name of Mary Wesley with joy. Not long after her birth, either by carelessness of her nurse or through an unfortunate accident, she was seriously injured and became a cripple for life. She was born at South Ormsby about 1696. There is no extant record of her baptism, but she was probably baptised by her own father, rector at the time, of the South Ormsby parish.

Early in 1697 the Wesley family moved to the living at Epworth, and here the rest of her brothers and sisters were born. Mary or "Molly" as she was called, soon discovered that she was "different." The neighborhood children and their parents jeered at her because of her infirmity. Her own brothers and sisters laughed at her. Even Susanna, her mother, thought she was somewhat dull because she required a day and a half to learn her letters perfectly, whereas all of her sisters and her brother had accomplished this feat in one day. Later her mother modified her opinion.

Mary, herself, referred to the difficulties she had faced in her childhood in a letter written to her brother John when she was about thirty years old.

> . . . but since God has cut me off from the pleasureable parts of life, and rendered me incapable of attracting the love of my relations, I must use my utmost endeavor to secure an eternal happiness, and he who is no respector of persons will require no more than he has given. You may now think that I am uncharitable in blaming my relations for want of affection, and I should readily agree with you had I not convincing reasons to the contrary; one of which, and I think an undeniable one, is this, that I have always been the jest of the family—and it is not I alone who make this observation, for then it might very well be attributed to my suspicion—but here I will leave it and tell you some news. (Stev, p. 290)

She then turns to other topics. A Mary Owran has been married and "we only wanted your company to make us completely merry; for who can be sad where you are?" She asks for some silk so that she can knit him another pair of gloves and then continues to tell him the neighborhood and family news to complete a most delightful letter.

Mary was correct in her appraisal of the general attitude of the family toward her. She was not feeling sorry for herself. Nor was she imagining what had happened. Charles, her brother, writing to John about this time, refers to Mary as "a patient Grizzle like Moll." (Stev, p. 291) Charles was probably writing playfully and not unkindly, but his remark bears out Mary's contention that she was "the jest of the family."

However, one by one the members of the family learned to respect her; partly because of the beauty of her spirit and partly because of the kindliness of her nature. Eventually, she came to be considered, at least by the biographers of the Wesley family, as one of the sweetest, purest, happiest and least hypocritical of all the Wesley family. Her name became synonymous with joy.

Mary's sister Mehetabel or "Hetty" was probably the first to discover the true depths of Mary's soul. Hetty, in her youth, rebelled against her parents, eloped to London with a lawyer, only to find that he wanted her as a mistress and not a wife. She returned to Epworth after one night with her lover to find she was deeply disgraced in the eyes of the entire family, except in the eyes of Mary and possibly John. (See Chapter Five.)

Hetty, in her despair, rashly vowed to marry the first man who would have her. She found a suitor all too soon in an uncouth plumber named Wright. He was totally incompatible with a person of Hetty's culture and education, and she backed away from her resolution. But Hetty's father, who probably had arranged the match, insisted that she keep her vow, and Hetty felt that because she had sinned so deeply this was the only way she could demonstrate her repentance. Mary, who loved her sister, urged her not to take such a fatal step. It seemed as though the entire immediate family of the Wesleys, except Mary, stood ready to cast the first stone. Mary's conduct was like a diamond without a flaw. Hetty, herself, years later remembered the kindness of her sister in a poem to her memory published in *The Gentleman's Magazine*:

> . . .
> From earliest dawn of youth, in thee well known
> The saint sublime and finished Christian shown:
> Yet would not grace one grain of pride allow,
> Or cry, "Stand off, I'm holier than thou."
> A worth so singular since time began,
> But One surpassed and He was more than man.
> When deep immersed in griefs beyond redress,
> And friend and kindred heightened my distress,
> And with relentless effort made me prove
> Pain, grief, despair, and wedlock without love;
> My soft Maria could alone dissent,
> O'relooked the fatal vow, and mourned the punishment!
> (Stev, p. 295)

It must have required a great deal of courage on the part of Mary, the beautiful cripple, to stand out against both her father and mother. Her mother's tight-lipped opposition had broken the will of Emily when she would have continued her relationship with Robert Leybourne, and the rector's wrath could be terrifying. He had once publicly rebuked a British army officer for his vile language, and the officer had backed down. On another occasion he had supported an unpopular candidate at an election, and he had withstood an unruly mob that demonstrated all night in front of the rectory where there was little or no police protection. Mr. Wesley, himself, was a man of great personal courage and a fiery temper, and for Mary to face him, at this moment, took an even greater courage. But Mary was equal to the challenge. She was as high-spirited as any of the Wesleys, and when she knew she was right, she had no fear in going forward or taking her stand.

In her poem to her sister, Hetty also gives a graphic description of Mary's beautiful white complexion, black eyes and kindly soul and spirit:

> . . .
> Witness thy brow, begnignant, clear,
> That none could doubt transcendent truth dwelt there.
> Witness the taintless whiteness of thy skin,
> Pure emblem of the purer soul within —
> That soul which, tender, unassuming, mild,
> Through jetty eyes with tranquil sweetness smiled.
> But ah! could fancy paint, or language speak,
> The roseate beauties of thy lip or cheek
> Where nature's pencil, leaving art no room,
> Touched to a miracle the vernal bloom.
> (Stev, p. 295)

These verses are written in the rigid style of the eighteenth century and are exceedingly sentimental. However, they demonstrate that Hetty found in Mary not someone to laugh at or jest about, but a true and faithful friend.

Adam Clark, a Methodist preacher and a friend of both John and Charles Wesley in their maturity, writes this about Mary:

> . . . all written and oral testimony concurs in the statement that her face was exceedingly beautiful, and was a fair and legible index to a mind and disposition almost angelic. Mr. John and Charles Wesley frequently spoke of her, and ever with the most tender respect; and her sister *Hetty,* no mean judge of character, with whom she was an especial favorite, spoke and wrote of her as one of the most exalted of human characters. (Clarke, p. 472)

Slowly the family had come to realize that Mary was one of those persons who are infrequently placed upon this earth to give humankind a beauty it could never otherwise possess.

Her father also began to appreciate Mary, but for a more practical reason. In a letter to John dated September 5, 1728, he writes in evident pride of Mary's earning capacity:

> M[olly] miraculously gets money, even in Wroot, and has given the first-fruits of her earnings to her mother, lending her money, and presenting

her with a new cloak of her own buying and making—for which God will bless her. When we get to Epworth [the family evidently was living for a time at Wroot] she will grow monstrously rich, for she will have more work than she can do, and the people are monstrously civil.

(JWL, I, p. 233)

With a characteristic generosity Mary was aiding with the household expenses which pleased the rector greatly.

There are few extant letters of Mary Wesley. She probably wrote many more than we have, but no one places much value on the letters of "the family jest." John, however, kept the two that have been recorded in Stevenson's *Memorials of the Wesley Family*. They make delightful reading. Mary speaks about her activities and the news of the parish; she then discusses more profound themes, which reveal the keenness of her mind and her grasp upon her theological ideas.

However, because of her physical handicap, Mary probably never expected that anyone would seek her hand in marriage. It is unlikely that any of the young men of Epworth or Wroot or the surrounding neighborhood were interested in her in spite of her beautiful face and smooth complexion. In a sense she was the family drudge. There is little doubt she longed to be loved. More than her sisters, her own gentle, loving soul reached out for a worthy partner. Eventually her search centered on a most unlikely youth named Johnny Whitelamb, who joined the Wesley family in 1727 to help Samuel, Sr. with his commentary on the book of Job.

Johnny Whitelamb

Johnny Whitelamb was a tall, gangling youth, the son of poor parents living in the neighborhood of Wroot. Born in 1710 he was about fourteen years younger than Mary.

Wroot, itself, was situated upon an eminence surrounded by a marsh, and, at certain times of the year, it was accessible only by boat. Eventually the parish became attached to the work at Epworth, with Samuel Wesley serving and sometimes living at both places. About the time of Johnny's birth, three charity schools had been established: one at Wroot, one at Hatfield, and one at Thorne. When Johnny became old enough he was sent to the charity school at Wroot. Here he was taught to read and write and received instruction in the Bible and Catechism. He probably met Samuel Wesley, Sr. through John Romley, Wesley's curate for a time, and principal of the school at Wroot. Wesley was so impressed by Whitelamb's deportment and his eager desire to learn that, about the year 1727 he took him into his own home. In this way Whitelamb met Mary Wesley, whom he soon worshipped from afar. However, without any family background or education, he could hardly hope to seek much less win the hand of a Wesley. In addition, he was fourteen years Mary's junior.

When Johnny came to Epworth, the doughty rector was working on his greatest scholarly production—his *Dissertationes in Librum Jobi*. The young student served as Samuel's amanuensis for the next four years. He carefully made a fair copy of the Dissertation for the publisher and added some line drawings and engravings. In addition Mr. Wesley began, rather sporadically, to instruct him in theological and classical studies.

However, as Dr. Richard Heitzenrater, one of the world's leading Wesleyan scholars, pointed out in an article in the *Proceedings of the Wesley Historical Society*, this somewhat idyllic picture needs considerable modification. There was far more tension in the Wesley household than we might imagine. On the authority of a letter from Whitelamb to Mrs. Wesley, Dr. Heitzenrater writes:

> Johnny was at first "extremely glad" to live with "so pious a family", but his four years in the Epworth rectory were marked by increasing tensions and uneasiness. He left his work more than once, claiming that he was being branded as "the most odious of all characters, . . . deprecated and reviled by every common servant." On one occasion of truancy in 1730, he wrote to Susanna, listing the disadvantages under which he was working: the likelihood of no recompense or: "future advantage", it not being in Mr. Wesley's power to provide such; the constant struggle with Samuel's temper and his "satirical wit"; the "poor and wretched condition" to which he had been reduced for want of clothes, exposing him to universal contempt and bringing grief to his own mother; and—worst of all, in his mind—that "my master has learned me nothing". (Heit, MWM, p. 155)

Nevertheless, Whitelamb, after each period of absence, would again return to the rectory to resume his "flail", as he called it.

Whitelamb's plight was certainly lamentable, although probably somewhat exaggerated. Nevertheless, it served one good purpose—it brought Johnny closer to Mary Wesley. She seemed to understand his frustration and despair as no one else. Even as Johnny apparently had been the butt of Samuel's satirical wit, so Mary had been "the family jest." She knew what it meant to be laughed at. She began to take an interest in Johnny's work. In fact, she began to work with him on her father's project. She soon became so involved with Johnny and his work that her sister Patty explained in a letter to her brothers at Oxford (probably with her tongue in her cheek) that Molly was so busy working for Johnny Whitelamb she would probably have no time to write to them.

Maybe Whitelamb had become discouraged and felt himself badly used because, having one time saved the life of his mentor, he was hoping for some tangible expression of gratefulness which was not immediately forthcoming. Samuel Wesley, himself, records the story of his rescue in a letter to his son John dated September 5, 1728:

God has given me fair escapes for life within these few weeks. The first was when my old nag fell with me, trailed me in the stirrups by one foot, and trod upon the other, yet never hurt me.

The other escape was much greater. On Monday week, at Burringham Ferry, we were driven down with a fierce stream and wind, and fell foul against a keel. Two of our horses were pitched overboard, and the boat was filled with water. I was just preparing to swim for life when John Whitelamb's long legs and arms swarmed up into the keel, and lugged me in after him. My mare was swimming a quarter of an hour; but, at last, we all got safe to land. Help to praise Him who saves both man and beast. (Ty, *SW*, p. 405)

However, eventually, and probably in realization of what they owed him, the Wesleys made it possible for Johnny to enter Lincoln College, Oxford. Samuel Wesley, Sr. may have provided some financial assistance, and Johnny co-operated by attempting to live well on three pence a day — which took some doing. In a letter to Samuel, Johnny reported on his progress and added a brief postscript sending his "humble service to Madame Wesley and Miss Molly"; to which Susanna responded in a letter to Charles, "Remember my love to poor starving Johnny." (Heit, MWM, p. 155)

At Oxford John Wesley became Whitelamb's tutor, finding him a hard-working student. In 1731 he said of him:

He reads one English, one Latin, and one Greek book alternately; and never meddles with a new one, in any of the languages, till he has ended the old one. If he goes on as he has begun, I dare take upon me to say that by the time he has been here four or five years, there will not be such a one, of his standing, in Lincoln College, perhaps not in the University of Oxford. (JWL, I, p. 282)

However, Whitelamb was still exceedingly poor. He could hardly dress properly. He badly needed a gown, and John Wesley interceded for him with his brother Samuel. Together they secured for the youth the much needed apparel. John had written to his brother:

John Whitelamb wants a gown much, and I am not rich enough to buy him one at present. If you are willing that my twenty shillings (that were) should go toward that, I will add ten to them, and let it lie till I have tried my interest with friends to make up the price of a new one. (JWL, I, p. 322)

Samuel replied:

I agree John Whitelamb shall have the money, on this condition, that he owns he has received the 20s in part of alleviation of my father's hard bargain with him, for I think it but just when he remembers the one should not forget the other — 'tis on my father's account that I consent. (JWL, I, p. 325)

Evidently Samuel Wesley, Sr. had made a bargain with Whitelamb which had never been fulfilled. Maybe he owed him money for acting as his amanuensis or for the sketches that appeared in the Rector's book on Job. It is difficult to say.

In addition, during his time at Oxford, Whitelamb was usually behind in his payments to the University. In 1732, on three different occasions, John Wesley was called to the bursar's office to help straighten out Whitelamb's financial problems.

During his last term at Oxford, Whitelamb became a further source of concern to Wesley by failing to conform to the disciplined life of the Methodists. One authority says, "He moved occasionally in doubtful company, and developed questionable views." (Green, p. 234) This may merely mean that he was attracted by Deism which offered a relief from the strict views and practices of the Wesleys. However, Whitelamb swung back to his original stance, and in 1733 he was ordained, although he had not taken his degree. In the summer of the same year, while visiting at Epworth, Whitelamb's continuing interest in Molly Wesley developed to the point where he promised himself to her in what was known as a pre-engagement. Through correspondence and visits they had grown quite close by now, and their blossoming love had brought with it a new joy and happiness for both of them.

By August, Whitelamb was back once more at Oxford, this time deeply enmeshed in John Wesley's holy manner of living. He made a point of visiting his tutor's rooms every Sunday, Wednesday and Friday evenings for religious study and prayer. Usually both the Wesley brothers and a John Gambold were present in addition to William Smith, another student of Wesley's who was trying to live by Methodist rules.

On December 21, 1733 John Whitelamb, having written to Mary's father and secured his permission, married Molly Wesley with the whole-hearted approval of Samuel Wesley, Sr., but over the strong but silent objections of Mrs. Wesley and her daughter, Kezzy.

A Voice From the Past

Mrs. Wesley's and Kezzy's objection to the marriage of Mary and Johnny arose because of a story about Whitelamb that Kezzy had heard from her brother John. While Whitelamb was at Oxford and presumably in love with Mary and probably writing to her as often as opportunity afforded, he became attached to a Miss Betty. She seems to have been introduced to him by a man named Robinson whom Mrs. Wesley later called a pimp, but who was in reality another of Wesley's students. Apparently little is known about Miss Betty, or how deeply Johnny became involved with her. John Wesley found out about the affair through William Smith. Whitelamb and Smith were both members of the group which met with the Wesley brothers and Gambold each week for Bible study and prayer. How Smith discovered the affair between Miss Betty and Whitelamb we have no way of knowing. His reporting of the matter to Wesley would seem today like an invasion of Whitelamb's privacy. However, both men were a part of Wesley's Holy Club and were attempting to supervise each other's conduct. Smith, probably, had no desire to confront Whitelamb directly with what he had discovered, and so he reported the matter to John Wesley, his tutor, leaving him to decide what was to be done.

After talking the matter over with several other persons, John Wesley tried to talk with Miss Betty. However, he was unable to contact Miss Betty or her sister Sally Lumley, who fled when she saw Wesley approaching. Eventually Wesley talked with both Whitelamb and Miss Betty and learned "All", whatever that expression of Wesley's may mean.

It is clear that Miss Betty was socially unsuited to become the wife of a clergyman, and it may be that Whitelamb never intended the matter to go as far as it did. The whole affair might have ended quietly had not Wesley dug into it. At any rate, after this confrontation, Wesley and Johnny proceeded to Epworth where Wesley very soon related the whole story to Kezzy. Her only reply was that Mary must be told! Accordingly Mary was told! She did not seem unduly alarmed by the story and her relationship with Johnny continued without interruption. Wesley was very happy that Mary took the matter so calmly and that the affair had ended so peacefully. He wrote in his diary *Vortat Bene* — it turned out well.

However, things were not as peaceful as they seemed. In letters written by Mrs. Wesley and by Kezzy to Wesley, himself, *after* Mary was married to John Whitelamb, there is set forth a series of dramatic episodes that occurred after Wesley returned to Oxford, leaving John Whitelamb for a time at Epworth.

The story of Whitelamb's indiscretion, unfortunately, did not remain a secret very long. Kezzy, herself, admits to repeating it to Patty and possibly others. Sooner or later the matter was sure to come to Mrs. Wesley's knowledge, although her husband was never apprised of what was going on. Mrs. Wesley claimed that Molly, herself, told her the story, although this seems unlikely. There apparently was so much tale-bearing going on that it is difficult to be sure who told whom. The Wesleys were never great ones for keeping confidences.

Mrs. Wesley further insisted that Whitelamb, himself, boasted of the affair in the presence of both Molly and Kezzy. This, too, seems unlikely. However, something of the kind may have happened. Possibly after Kezzy and John told Mary of Johnny's one wild oat they may have confronted him with the story; and he may have displayed pride instead of shame in having attracted the affections of the beautiful (?) Miss Betty. After all, Johnny had always been looked down upon by the Wesley family, and here was his chance to show that he was not as unattractive a "catch" as some might have imagined.

Later, however, Mrs. Wesley took a hand in this strange game of love. In describing to John Wesley her part in the matter, she wrote:

> . . . Indeed when he came hither first, he was so full of his new Doxy that he could not forbear telling Molly and Kezzy of his armour, which the former informed me of; and I discoursed him about it, and would have convinced him that it was sinful, and dishonourable for him to court another woman when he was pre-ingaged. He was not much moved with what I could say. So I told him plainly, he should presently renounce one or the other, and that if he did not presently write to Robinson (who is his pimp) and tell him that he would never more have any conversation with his doll at Medley, I would immediately send Molly away, where he should never see her more; though withall, I advised him rather to take his Betty than your sister, for I thought her a much fitter wife for him. Besides, I was extremely unwilling Molly should ever marry at all. But Molly, who was fond of him to the last degree, was of another mind, and persuaded him to write to Robinson and show me the letter. I did not much approve it, because he seemed to justify those vile practices which I thought he ought to have condemned. Yet to satisfy her importunity I permitted them to go on. Whitelamb wrote to ask your father leave to marry his daughter, which Mr. Wesley gave him, and on St. Thomas's Day married they were at Epworth by Mr. Horberry; full sore against my will, but my consent was never asked, and your father, brother Wesley &tc, being for the match, I said nothing against it to them, ... (Heit., MWM, P. 159)

Robinson was not a pimp, but another of Wesley's pupils who was quite concerned over the whole affair. However, in the eyes of Wesley, he did not lay it to heart—that is, consider the affair too seriously.

Kezzy also wrote a letter reprimanding Wesley for not labelling Whitelamb an immoral man. Up until the time of the actual wedding she apparently sought to dissuade Mary from the marriage without success. She tried every means but the one that would have surely stopped the nuptials—namely that of telling her father why in her mind Whitelamb was not a fit person to marry Mary.

There is, of course, another sidelight to the story. The speed with which Kezzy originally relayed the news of Whitelamb's indiscretion to her sister, Mary, suggests a more selfish motive on Kezzy's part than appears on the surface. Johnny was fourteen years younger than Mary, and nearer Kezzy's age. Is it possible that Kezzy, herself, was in love with Johnny? And can it be that she could not understand why Johnny did not prefer her to Mary who was a cripple and the "jest of the family"? It is hard to say. Certainly both John Wesley and Kezzy demonstrated a total lack of sensitivity in hurrying to Mary with the story. It would have been better had John dropped the whole matter when he and Whitelamb left Oxford for Epworth. But maybe Wesley was aware of Kezzy's affection for Johnny. Earlier John Wesley had visited Kezzy when she was teaching and studying in a school at Lincoln. He had talked with Kezzy about Johnny Whitelamb, a talk which he says left her "calm", whatever that means. It should be remembered also that John Wesley often gave far greater importance to passing events than they deserved. He loved to meddle in people's lives. He was the eternal tinkerer with souls. After he had spoken of the affair with Mary he thought he had settled the matter very satisfactorily. He had apparently forgotten about Kezzy or the effect the situation might have on her, and what might happen if the matter came to the attention of his parents. The interplay of the personalities presents a curious puzzle. There is, however, little doubt that, whatever faults there may have been on the part of anyone, Mary and Johnny loved each other deeply.

In the end, the only one who was especially upset was Johnny Whitelamb who forever afterward carried a deep grudge against Kezzy. Some time later, when, as we shall see, Kezzy was being courted by Westley Hall, Whitelamb wrote a devastating letter to Hall concerning Kezzy's character. It astounded even John Wesley to whom Hall showed the letter. If it doubtful if Johnny ever forgave Kezzy for her part in the affair. It is doubtful if he ever forgot that Kezzy alone tried to the very last to dissuade Mary from marrying him.

Opportunity and Tragedy

On January 14, 1734 Samuel Wesley, Sr. wrote a letter to the Lord Chancellor requesting him to transfer the living at Wroot from himself to John Whitelamb. In his letter the Rector outlined Whitelamb's early life, his training under Samuel Wesley, himself, and his record at Oxford including his ordination as a deacon. He added, "I gave my consent to his marrying one of my seven daughters." He then points out that Wroot is not a particularly desirable living, "not wanting in water" — obviously a reference to the marshy condition of the land, "but *they* love the place, though I can get no body else to reside on it."

He closes his letter by describing Whitelamb as indeed

> . . . a valuable person, of uncommon brightness, learning, piety, and indefatigable industry; always loyal to the King, zealous for the Church, and friendly to our dissenting brethren. For the truth of his character I will be answerable to God and man. (Ty, *OM*, p. 377)

The Rector's request was seriously considered, and in *The Gentleman's Magazine* for the month of February 1734 there appeared the following notice in the list of ecclesiastical preferments: "Mr. Whitelamb to the rectory of Wroot, Lincolnshire."

The joy of Mary and Johnny Whitelamb was full. Forgotten now were the unpleasant scenes at Epworth and John's indiscretion at Oxford. Mary and Johnny loved Wroot with its great marshes and wide skies; they loved the birds that nested in the marsh; they loved the rectory, small and mean as it may have seemed to others; but most of all they loved each other and their God. Their love and joy was boundless. Mary's search for love was ended; or, in another view, just beginning.

We know little of the life of Mary and Johnny at Wroot, other than they took great pains with their work. They neglected no one, they shirked no duty, they fulfilled the work of the ministry as one person. Tragedy, however, struck down their happiness as a lightning bolt fells a tree during a summer storm. Mary died in childbirth in October 1734, less than a year after the two occupied the rectory at Wroot. Mary had a long, difficult labor and she survived her still born baby by only a day or two. In the list of burials for that year there appears in the Parish Register at Wroot a simple entry that embodies one of life's inexplicable cruelties: "1734, November 1st, Mrs. Whitelamb, wife of Mr. Whitelamb." Then follows the signature, "John Whitelamb, rector."

For a time John Whitelamb's sorrow was so great his friends thought he would go out of his mind. Samuel Wesley, Sr. was sure the youth would follow Mary to the grave. He tried to assuage Whitelamb's grief by a new challenge, and he told him of the plans of Charles and John, his sons, who were considering serving as missionaries to the Indians in Georgia in the New World. Whitelamb was interested. But for some reason not recorded he either backed out of the venture or was unable to secure permission to serve. Maybe he could not bear the thought of leaving the church at Wroot where all that was earthly of his Mary was buried. Maybe he felt a special responsibility to his parishioners who, crude as they were, had probably been very kind to him during his great sorrow. Whitelamb remained at Wroot for thirty-five years, and when he died not only his parishioners but also many neighboring clergymen came to his funeral. He had made a deep impression on his parish and the surrounding community.

Unfortunately, with the death of Mary, the Wesleys, with the exception of one incident, seem to have ostracized Whitelamb.

In June of 1742 John Wesley was in the vicinity of Wroot and Epworth. At seven that morning he preached in the neighboring parish of Haxey. Then he writes:

> I went to Wroot, of which (as well as Epworth) my father was rector for several years. Mr. Whitelamb offering me the church, I preached in the morning on "Ask and it shall be given you"; in the afternoon, on the difference between the righteousness of the law and the righteousness of faith. But the church could not contain the people, many of whom came from afar; and, I trust, not in vain. (JWJ, Vol. 3, p. 24)

A week before, Wesley had sought permission to preach at Epworth, but John Romley, the Rector, refused his request. As a result, Wesley announced through a friend he would preach at six o'clock from his father's tombstone

From AN ALBUM OF METHODIST HISTORY
by Elmer T. Clark

Courtesy of the
Abingdon Press

Wroot Church (above) and Wroot Rectory (below) where Mary Wesley (Mrs. John Whitelamb) lived and served for one happy year before her death in childbirth in 1734. Her husband continued to serve the parish until his death in 1769.

in the churchyard. A great crowd gathered. As a result, Wesley preached from his father's tombstone every evening in the week, always drawing a large crowd. However, he probably preached only one more time at Wroot, possibly because the Wroot people were not too happy with the arrangement or maybe because Whitelamb was uneasy at the possible reaction of his superiors who did not all favor Wesley.

Whitelamb, however, was deeply hurt because the Wesleys would have little or nothing to do with him. He wrote a letter to John stating his gratefulness for the help given him by the Wesley family and asking why they had now forsaken him. He never received a satisfactory reply. Apparently none of the Wesleys ever fully forgave Whitelamb for his conduct with Miss Betty — an incident which Whitelamb later, in a letter to Charles Wesley, said stemmed from "a heat of youthful blood and want of experience in the world." (Arminian Magazine, 1778, p. 186) Probably also the Wesleys disapproved of his leaning toward Deism and later toward Catholicism. In addition, Whitelamb had lost his Methodist zeal and faith. This possibly was another reason for the attitude of the Wesleys. It is hard to say.

What had been sown in joy had been reaped in sorrow. Mary Wesley, the only one of the Wesley sisters who knew the fullest depth of love and joy in this life, was cut off at high noon, and the man who loved her ended his days in loneliness.

He died in the month of July in the year 1769. After his death, Wesley took a belated interest in him. He wrote to a Mrs. Woodhouse for information on the cause of death, and whether Whitelamb had been ill for any length of time. Then he ungraciously added, "Oh why did he not die forty years ago while he knew in whom he believed!" (JWLT, Vol. 5, p. 151) That is, while he was a Methodist.

Wesley, of course, was Wesley! But Whitelamb must have made some impact for good on his community for someone inscribed on his tombstone the words, "Worthy of Imitation." Obviously, none of the Wesleys attended Whitelamb's funeral.

At Molly's death, however, four of the Wesleys at least, had expressed his or her sorrow in his or her own way. Samuel, Jr. wrote a eulogy. Charles requested the eulogy from Samuel for preservation, but there are no extant copies, and the work may never have been published. John wrote a memorial sermon. It seems never to have been published. Hetty, Mary's sister, who loved Mary dearly, if for no other reason than that Mary had stood boldly against her sisters and parents to protect her, wrote an Epitaph. It has been preserved, having been published in *The Gentleman's Magazine,* but was never inscribed on the plaque in the church at Wroot where Mary was buried.

Epitaph on Mrs. Mary Whitelamb

If highest worth, in beauty's bloom,
Exempted mortals from the Tomb,
We had not round this sacred Bier
Mourned the sweet Babe and Mother here,
Where innocence from harm is blest,
And the meek sufferer is at rest!
Fierce pangs she bore without complaint,
Till heaven relieved the finish'd Saint.

If savage bosoms felt her woe
(Who lived and died without a foe,)
How should I mourn, or how commend,
My tenderest, dearest, *firmest* friend?
Most pious, meek, resign'd, and chaste,
With every social virtue graced!

If, Reader, thou wouldst prove, and know,
The ease she found not here below;
Her bright example points the way
To perfect bliss and endless day.

(Clarke, p. 480)

Chapter Five

Passion and Punishment
The Story of Mehetabel Wesley

Mrs. William Wright

Childhood and Youth

Hetty Wesley's search for love is the most heart-breaking story of the seven sisters. To tell the tale in its entirety, with its sordid revelation of human nature, would require the narrative gifts of a Dickens, the psychological insight of a Hawthorne, and the structural ability of a DeMaupassant. In some ways, Hetty's story was a common occurrence in the eighteenth century, and in other ways it was so preposterous as to lack credibility.

Hetty Wesley was the first child born to Susanna and Samuel Wesley, Sr., after they settled in the rectory at Epworth. They had moved here from South Ormsby. Seven children had previously been born, four of whom grew to maturity and three of whom died in infancy. The exact date of Hetty's birth is not known, although she was probably born in the year 1697 or 1698. There is no extant record of her baptism. She was named Mehetabel, nicknamed "Hetty" and sometimes called "Kitty" by her older brother, Samuel, Jr.

She was gifted with a warm, happy personality and a brilliant mind. By the time she was eight years of age she could read her New Testament in Greek. She was probably the most beautiful of the Wesley sisters. She was well-shaped, with trim ankles, a narrow waist, and firm, full breasts. She had a serene countenance, merry eyes, and a ready smile that quickly burst into musical laughter. One of her biographers wrote, "nearly all the graces and gifts of her brothers and sisters were combined in her personal appearance, accomplishments, and mental endowments." (Stev, p. 298) Adam Clarke, who wrote one of the earliest biographies of the Wesley family, makes reference to Hetty as "sprightly; full of mirth, good humour, and keen wit." (Clarke, p. 487)

Her childhood must have been a happy one. The home life of the Wesleys was well ordered, and family forms of entertainment interspersed lengthy periods of school and study. The Wesleys played cards and enjoyed dancing. Some of the Wesleys loved to hike through the fields and marshes, picking flowers and berries, and all of them read as avidly as teenagers today follow television programs. Doubtless, Hetty entered into all these diversions. She was probably the best card player and the most graceful dancer of the Wesley family. In addition, the household chores were carried out in a lively, happy manner. Samuel Wesley, Jr. wrote a charming poem picturing his sisters performing these daily tasks. (See Chapter Two, p. 15)

He actually wrote the poem for Hetty, whom he describes as "sober." He may have been teasing, for the testimony of all other witnesses is that Hetty was far from "sober" and that her wit and humour did much to bring a spirit of merriment to the Wesley household.

Possibly Hetty's precociousness was indirectly aided by the rectory fire in 1709. She was only about twelve years of age at the time. She had been awakened when some burning brands fell upon her bed. She arose with a scream, and shortly after heard the yell of "Fire!" in the streets. She called to her mother and then, together with Martha, hurried to the first floor of the house, where they found the manservant, Harry, in the parlor. He smashed a window, bodily lifted the two girls in his arms, and pushing them through the broken frame, placed them in the garden. Here they soon joined the remainder of the family, including John, who was only five years of age. He was rescued at the last minute from the second floor by several alert neighbors who formed a human ladder and swung little "Jacky" out of harm's way just as the roof of the rectory collapsed.

For the next several months the Wesley children were placed in the homes of friends and relatives. Martha and Hetty went to live with their Uncle Matthew in London. He was their father's brother. Matthew was popular with his friends, urbane in his manners, gentle in his ministrations to the Wesley family, and annoyed to distraction by the inability of his brother, Samuel, Sr. properly to manage his financial affairs.

In her Uncle Matthew's house Hetty met a different kind of person than those she had met in Epworth or Wroot. Here were students, gentlemen and ladies whose polished manners imparted to Hetty, herself, young as she was, a bearing and sophistication more in keeping with her keen mind, physical beauty and ready wit than any training she had experienced at home.

When she returned to Epworth, her life continued much as it had before her sojourn in London. Her mother noted the changes in the conduct of the children, and she quickly tightened the reins of parental authority to secure obedience to her rules once more. She was, as usual, successful.

Early Suitors

There is little doubt that the young men of Epworth and Wroot clustered around the sisters, but especially around Hetty. She must have attracted the country swains as a stage star attracts wealthy admirers. Some of them possibly proposed marriage; but if there were any proposals, they were swept aside by Hetty's iron-willed father, Samuel, Sr.

At the time when "Old Jeffrey" haunted the Wesley rectory, Emily, Hetty's oldest sister, noted as we have seen that their father thought the noises were made by the village swains visiting his older daughters. Hetty was about nineteen years of age at the time, and it is easy to believe that between her laughter and the muffled voices of her lovers, some persons might have thought the rectory was haunted. Further events, however, revealed that there was not the slightest connection between the evening visitors and the ghost. The poltergeist had a personality of its own, and it was indebted to no human agency for assistance.

For a time some biographers thought that the hauntings were a hoax perpetuated by Hetty, herself—Hetty the mischievous, Hetty the brilliant, whose fertile brain could have concocted such a scheme of events as might be laid to a ghost.

This theory was enhanced by the fact that there is no record of the hauntings written by Hetty. Her narrative, if it ever existed, was presumably lost. But this is difficult to believe. John Wesley, himself, collected the accounts— one from each member of the family who had experienced the nocturnal and sometimes daytime visits of "Old Jeffrey," the poltergeist. John would hardly have mislaid his sister's account. He was not a careless man. He had collected the narratives with a view to publication, later printing them in *The Arminian Magazine.*

Other authorities suggest that Hetty refused to set forth her version because she knew too much, and she was afraid her narrative might corroborate the suspicion that she was the ghost.

This also is an unlikely conclusion. The rappings and the noises were heard sometimes when Hetty was asleep or in another part of the house, or present under the watchful eyes of her mother and sisters. Of all the sisters, she was the most troubled by the ghost, sometimes crying out in her sleep or trembling as if in an ague. Like her sisters, however, she soon became accustomed to the antics of "Old Jeffrey" and refused to be worried about what was happening.

She was concerned, however, that her father was sweeping aside the advances of even those more acceptable lovers who paid Hetty attention. Maybe the rector, in a fatherly sort of way, was jealous of his daughter and her suitors. No one, he thought, was quite good enough for her. She was his most brilliant daughter and had often acted as his amanuensis. The thought of giving her up to a local farmer, however prosperous, was inconceivable to him. His attitude troubled Hetty, and she wrote a short poem to her mother, ending with these poignant lines:

> Pray speak a word in time of need
> And with my sour-looked father plead
> For your distressed daughter!
> (Stev, p. 299)

It was one of her first attempts at poetry, but it apparently did little good. Later in life Hetty would seek to perfect her poetic talent, and some of her work would be published in several family magazines in addition to *The Gentleman's Magazine,* a prestigious publication of eighteenth century

The Gentleman's Magazine:

Lond Gazette
Lond Journ
Fog's Journ.
Applebee's ::
Read's : : : :
Craftsman :
D. Spectator;
Grubstreet J
Free-Briton
Hyp: Doctor
Daily Cour.
Daily Post;
Dai. Journal
Da. Post-boy
D. Advertiser
Evening Post
St James's Eh.
Whitehall Eb
Lond. Eveg
Weekly Misc
General &c.
Old Whig
Q. Gazetteer
Lon. D. Post

St John's Gate.

York News
Dublin 5 :::
Edinburgh 2
Bristol :::
Norwich 2
Exeter 2 ::
Worcester : :
Northampton
Gloucester : :
Stamford ::
Nottingham
Salisp Journ.
Chester bitto
Derby bitto
Ipswich do.
Reading do.
Leeds Merc.
Newcastle ll
Canterbury
Durham
Kendal
Boston : : ¶
Jamaica &c
Barbados :

For MARCH, 1736.

CONTAINING,

/more in Quantity, and greater Variety, than any Book of the kind and Price/

I. ORIGINAL Letters and Dissertations: 1. On a Note in the Odyssey. 2. The Philosopher's Prayer. 3. The Summary of Natural Religion. 4. The Doctrine of Abstinence from Blood. 5. On Epigrams. 6. A Critique on *Saul*, a Tragedy. 7. Lunar Eclipses.

II. ESSAYS on various Subjects; (*viz.*) On Witches and Witchcraft. On Dancing. On Nonsense. Friendship. Long Noses. Proposal for a new Colony.

III. POLITICAL Points. The fatal Consequence of Ministerial Influence. Importance of *Lorrain*. On the Plan of Peace. K *Stanislaus's* Abdication. *Jeremiac* Writers. Of giving Air to public Assemblies. Excellence of Lord *Bolingbroke*. Dissenters made Tools. Indulgence of the Toleration Act.

IV. THEOLOGICAL Points. Of the Test Act. Plain Account of the Sacrament. Particular Providence. A Call to the Country *Dissenters*.

V. LIST of the small Livings augmented by Q. *Anne's* Bounty, *&c.* in 1735. The *Irish* House of Commons Resolutions against new Tythes.

VI. POETRY, most Originals. Prize-Epigrams, a Despairing Lady's dying Farewell, *&c.* (*See Contents.*)

VII. HISTORICAL Passages, foreign and domestic. Petitions to Parliament. Cotton Manufacture.

VIII. LISTS of Births, Marriages, Promotions Civil and Military, Bankrupts, Deaths.

IX. PRICE of Stocks. Bill of Mortality. Forty Pounds in Prizes.

X. REGISTER of Books.

XI. TABLE of Contents.

By SYLVANUS URBAN, Gent.

LONDON: Printed by E. CAVE at St JOHN's GATE, and Sold by the Booksellers of Town and Country; of whom may be had any former Month. Note, *The Debates and Proceedings in Parliament inserted in this Collection are fuller than in any other. See Supplement to the Gentleman's Magazine,* 1735.

Courtesy of the Library Company, Philadelphia

Cover of THE GENTLEMAN'S MAGAZINE, one of the most prestigious magazines of 18th Century England. The March 1736 issue carried a laudatory poem by "Silvius" praising the manuscript poems of Mehetabel Wesley (Mrs. William Wright) which can be seen on the opposite page in the upper left hand corner.

Poetical ESSAYS; MARCH 1736.   155

To Mrs W——T on reading her Manuscript
POEMS.

FAIN wou'd my grateful muse a trophy raise,
   Devoted to *Granvilla*'s lasting praise,
But from what topick shall her task begin?
From outward charms or richer stores within?
'Twere difficult with *Pourtrait* just to trace,   5
The blooming beauties of her lovely face,
The roseat bloom that blushes on her cheek,
Her eyes, whence rays of pointed light'ning break,
Each brow, the bow of *Cupid*, whence his darts
With cer ain arch'ry strike unguarded hearts,   10
Her lips, that with a rubied tincture glow,
Soft as the soothing sounds which from 'em flow:
But oh! what words! what numbers shall I find,
T' express the boundless treasures of her mind?
Where wit and judgment spread their copious
And ev'ry grace, and ev'ry virtue shines. (mines,
O nymph, when you assume the muses' lyre,
What thoughts you quicken, and what joys inspire?
Pale melancholy wears a cheerful mien,
Grief smiles, and raging passions grow serene. 20
If themes sublime, of import grand, you try,
You lift th' attentive spirit to the sky,
Or change the strain and sportive subjects chuse,
Our soft'ning souls obey thy pow'rful muse.
Yet 'tis, *Granvilla*, not thy smallest praise,
That no indecent thought profanes thy lays,
Like thy own breast thy style from taint is free,
Censure may pry, but can no blemish see;
No longer let thy muse the press decline?
Publish her lays, and prove her race divine; 30
Long has thy tuneful *sire* been known to fame,
On him *Maria* smil'd, a royal name:
Thy *brother*'s works, receiv'd with rapture, tell
That on the son, the father's spirit fell:
To these the *daughter*'s equal flame adjoin,
Then boast, O muses, the unrival'd *line*.

PRIZE-EPIGRAM 1.   SYLVIUS.

ALLOW'D by bright *Granvilla* to peruse
   The sprightly labours of her charming muse,
Enraptur'd by her wit's inspiring rays,
I chaunted ready numbers to her praise;
She, pleas'd, my unpremeditated lines,
To the recording Magazine consigns:
But wou'd you be to best advantage known?
Print not my verses, fairest, but your own.

PRIZE-EPIGRAM 2.   SYLVIUS.

VAPRISSA, of sickness, complain'd to
      a friend,
And 'twas quickly between them agreed,
That the languishing nymph was approaching
So a doctor was sent for with speed; (her end,
He felt her pulse, and examin'd her urine,
Yet nought from the symptoms cou'd tell her.
But this—he was sure the distemper of—curing,
Cou'd he guess for his heart what shou'd ail her.

PRIZE-EPIGRAM 3.   SYLVIUS.

WHEN *Astrophil* provok'd the critic's rage,
   I judg'd the spleen auspicious to his page,
Discerning *Fido*'s skill was sure profound,
Dunce * *Astrophil* has won the *Fifty Pound*.

* See *Vol. V. p. 676. Col. 2. V. 34. 2nd*
Fido's other Epistles.

6

DAMON *to* PYTHIAS.

WHile far from toils your *Damon* sits secur'd
    From rustling storms and rattling hail
       immur'd;
While easy slumbers bless my downy bed,
And friends and health their softest influence shed;
While glowing fires correct the inclement sky,
And wife and children with their charms sit by;
Pathetic thoughts my *Pythias* still pursue,
Whom storms attack, and northern winds bedew.
The muse e'en shudders while she would rehearse
The toils you bear,—and rigours fill the verse.
   Fain would she follow with her wings out- ⎫
       spread,   ⎬
Fond of encircling that important head,   ⎭
And thinks she still could follow where you lead.
But ah! such flights her fancied powers exceed;
Affection prompts, but stronger wings she'll need.
Forward she springs to join her absent friend,
Eager thro' all his trav'ling toils to attend;
But see she struggling droops, with languor bends,
And all her sanguine hope in disappointment ends.
   But while I mourn the dreary wastes you tread,
Pause on your storms without a friendly shade,
While full of fears the spreading floods I view,
And sympathizing tears my cheeks bedew;
While exhalations clog the ambient air,
And on their wings unwholesome vapours bear;
While o'er the lonesome rocks and vales you pass,
O'erspread with frosts, and slippery as the glass,
With bended knee my ardent vows ascend,
That guardian angels may your steps attend;
In all your dangers lend their friendly arm,
To guide your doubtful way, secure from harm.
   When nature sickens, and the god of day
Is found too weak to drive the fogs away, [spread,
May these kind guards their friendly wings o'er-
Defend, support, and chear your drooping head;
Bid storms be calms, let zephyrs only rise,
With balmy wings to fan the foggy skies.——
   In vain the infant spring it's beauties sheds,
In vain sits brooding on the flow'ry beds,
Flora in vain enamels all my ground,
And ⅋ sweet primrose spreads its fragrance round; ⎫
In vain the violet, with its beauteous hue,   ⎬
Peeps out of nature's womb in mantle blue.   ⎭
All, all is nothing—till I hear of you.
   What tho' the airy songsters tune their throat,
And court mine ear ⅋ their once charming notes;
What tho' the lambkins, innocent and gay,
Frisk round me, and untaught their gambols play,
Methinks it's winter still, while sad I mourn,
That *Pythias* still protracts his wish'd return.

PRIZE-EPIGRAM 1.   LIBERUS.

On FIDELIA's *courting the* Dean, *and his silence.*

PHœbus no more the flying fair pursues,
   Nor *Sacharissa* fires a *Waller*'s muse,
But nymphs admire the god, and beauty-parts;
Apollo's wit, now best points *Cupid*'s darts.
So, cross the seas, *Fidelia* woo'd the *Dean*,
Shall two *Vanessa*'s sigh, and sigh in vain!
But tho' *Swift* wo'd not hear, wise *Phœbus* wo'd,
And to the fair soon flew the gladsome god;
At *Him* provok'd, no more inspires his lays,
But gives to *Her* the poetry and praise.

O 2

England. By that time, however, she would have gone through the fires of tragedy and her poetry would be written not in a light-hearted spirit, but in tears.

As Hetty matured, more and more young men became interested in her. Probably the most likely suitor was John Romley, then a school master at Wroot and Samuel Wesley's curate. He also acted, for a time, as his amanuensis.

He openly courted Hetty who became deeply enamoured of him. He was handsome, intelligent, of good family and had favourable prospects. When he asked for her hand in marriage, Hetty waited anxiously for her father's decision. The Rector, however, for no apparent reason, had taken a strong dislike to the young man. He may have heard some reports about Romley that distressed him. Possibly the Rector objected to Romley's alleged fondness for liquor, or maybe the Rector believed Romley to be careless — somewhat shiftless. It is hard to say what motivated Samuel Wesley's conduct. No adequate life of Samuel Wesley, Sr. has ever been written. Tyerman's *Life and Times of the Rev. Samual Wesley*, written in the nineteenth century, is the only authoritative biography of any scholarly standing, and it is outdated and at times inaccurate. Probably in a thoroughly researched life, Samuel Wesley would be less severely judged than he is by Quiller-Couch in his novel *Hetty Wesley*, or by Mrs. Nolan Harmon in her excellent study, *Susanna, Mother of the Wesleys*. At any rate, Samuel Wesley turned John Romley away, and then, possibly to make sure Romley and his daughter did not meet secretly, he secured a position for Hetty as a governess in the home of Mr. and Mrs. Grantham at Kelstein. He also may have wanted to help fill the void in Hetty's life (caused by the loss of Romley) with new surroundings in a family where she might possibly meet new friends. Romley never forgot this rejection, and in 1742, after he became rector at Epworth, he refused John Wesley permission to preach in his father's former pulpit.

From Governess to Lover

Hetty's work in the Grantham household was to serve as governess to two children and possibly as a companion to Mrs. Grantham. Her surroundings were pleasant and her appointments satisfactory. The Granthams were very kindly people, and they did their best to make Hetty feel at home; but their efforts were useless. One morning Hetty announced she was returning to Epworth. It is difficult to understand why Hetty left the Granthams so abruptly.

Dr. V. H. H. Green, in his study *The Young Mr. Wesley*, believed that all the Wesleys had been so trained that sooner or later they longed for the rectory at Epworth. They longed for home. It is an interesting idea, but untenable. Emily, the eldest Wesley sister, returned home only under the strongest pressure from her aging parents, particularly her mother. Martha came to hate her life at Epworth, and all the sisters seemed desirous of some form of marriage which would take them away from their father's house.

It is more likely that Hetty may have met at the Grantham's a young lawyer described by one biographer as "clever in his profession" and "of respectable family." (Stev, p. 302) When she met this youthful lawyer — who for some reason was never actually named either by Hetty or any member of her family — she fell in love with him. It is doubtful if the Granthams placed any restraints on Hetty as to the company she might keep, and it is difficult to imagine that they would have objected to the young man's attention to Hetty.

On the other hand, in spite of her mature years — Hetty was now in her late twenties — she would still wish for the blessing of her parents on any possible marriage. She would, therefore, have preferred to be courted at her home where she could aid in controlling her family's attitude toward this seemingly acceptable suitor. On the other hand, she may have wanted simply to think through her feelings for her new lover in light of her experience with Romley.

Whatever the purpose for returning home, she did not succeed in her ultimate purpose — to secure her father's permission to marry her new suitor. After examining the young man's background and conduct, Samuel, Sr. decided he was an "unprincipled lawyer" (Stev, p. 302) with a frivolous attitude toward life. He refused to allow the marriage.

It is difficult to understand the rector's attitude. Certainly he had reason enough to dislike lawyers, some of whom had probably hounded him about his debts; but this does not seem sufficient cause for turning away from his home a well-educated young man with good prospects. More likely he simply could not abide the thought of giving his daughter, Hetty, who was his prize student and his former amanuensis, to any man. Once having spoken, for him at least, the matter was ended.

Hetty was bitterly and uncontrollably disappointed. She apparently loved the man dearly; and to have him cast off in this manner seemed more than she could bear. She, therefore, continued meeting with him secretly and together they planned an elopement to London.

As the day for the elopement approached, Hetty was in an ecstacy of happiness. Where the lovers secretly met and how they made their way to London is not known. We can be sure, however, that the journey, possibly by stage-coach, to London with its constant traffic and thousands of people, its exotic tree-filled squares, and its numerous trade signs swinging and creaking in the wind must have caused Hetty's heart to beat rapidly with excitement. The warm feeling of the youthful, well-dressed lawyer by her side must have filled her spirit with a joy almost beyond her control. She was in love, and she was on her way to London and to marriage.

It would have been well had the couple gone to Hetty's Uncle Matthew for advice and help. He probably would have assisted in forwarding their plans. He had no great affection for his brother, Samuel, and would have had no reason to thwart Hetty's marriage. But Hetty and her lover went elsewhere. From what followed, it is reasonable to conclude that Hetty's friend, himself, may have objected to seeking Uncle Matthew's assistance.

In London Hetty faced the most crushing disappointment of her life. After spending the night with her lover, believing they would be married the next day, she discovered in the morning he had no intention of marrying her. It is difficult to understand why. It is hardly likely that he could have grown weary of her in one night. It is even less likely that he was, in this way, revenging himself on the entire Wesley family for their refusal of his suit. He may have seen Hetty more as a mistress than a bride, once he discovered her willingness to run off to London without her parent's consent, and to spend the night with him without the benefit of any kind of marriage ceremony or verbal contract. It is difficult to say.

Once she was certain of his duplicity, Hetty, confused and heart-broken, made the now long, wearisome journey back to Epworth and to her family for help and support. But here she faced an even greater disappointment. Hetty's father and mother and all her sisters, with the one exception of Mary as we have seen, turned against her. Hetty might have been bodily thrown out of the house had not her mother intervened. In her general attitude, however, Susanna stood with her husband and the rest of the household. John, Charles and Samuel, Jr. were in Oxford or London at the time, but they do not seem to have been of much help when they were apprised of the situation. They apparently joined the family in its general condemnation of Hetty, although their attitude, as did the attitude of some of Hetty's sisters, changed during the coming weeks and months.

At any rate, Hetty, in her poem *To the Memory of Mrs. Mary Whitelamb* (Mary's married name) written after Mary had died in 1734, makes it clear that only Mary stood by her in this hour of need and frustration (see Chapter Four).

Frightened at the thought that she might be pregnant — as she was — Hetty promised her father she would marry any suitor who would have her. Possibly at the instigation of the rector, himelf, a crude, uncouth but good-natured local plumber named William Wright appeared to claim Hetty's hand. When Hetty realized what kind of a match her father was arranging for her, she was horrified. She wanted to back away from her promise. Mary vehemently opposed the marriage. But Samuel insisted that Hetty had made a vow and had given her word to him, and the least she could do to save the family honor was to marry William Wright.

On October 13, 1725 the marriage took place, not at Epworth with her father presiding, but in the neighboring town of Haxey. The brilliant, beautiful, highly-educated, formerly happy Hetty became the wife of an uncouth, boorish, though good-natured man who later added drunkenness to his lifestyle. Hetty received a wedding present of five hundred pounds from her Uncle Matthew. There is no record, however, that any member of the Wesley family attended the ceremony or, aside from Uncle Matthew, demonstrated any love or support for the shaken, confused, sorrowful girl. Mary, being a cripple, probably had no way of attending the wedding by herself. However, Mary stayed close to Hetty, and when Hetty went to live with her husband at Louth, Mary went along to keep her company. How long she stayed is not known, but probably throughout the winter.

Wright had been originally from Louth, where his parents still lived, and where he was in business with his father. It was there — at Louth — that Hetty had her first child, a girl. The infant was baptised on February 18th, 1726 approximately four months after Hetty and Wright were married. The baby died and was buried at Louth December 27th, 1726. None of the Wesleys attended the funeral, except possibly Mary, who may still have been living with her sister.

For a time Wright continued in business with his father. Hetty did her best to make the marriage a happy one; but the treatment she was receiving from her own family was making the adjustment exceedingly difficult. The Wesleys were a close-knit group, and Hetty naturally longed for the family that had always been her support and comfort. Neither her father nor her mother would see Hetty. Their Puritan attitude proclaimed that Hetty had sinned and brought disgrace upon them. They doubted her repentance, and forgiveness without repentance was impossible.

The sincerity of her repentance, however, is demonstrated in that before her child was born, late in her pregnancy, Hetty made a hurried trip to Wroot in the hope of securing the forgiveness of her parents and family. She was unsuccessful. Mary described Hetty's visit to Wroot in a letter to Charles dated January 20th, 1726:

> My unhappy sister was at Wroote this week after you left us, where she stayed two or three days, and returned to Louth without seeing my father. Here I must stop unless I end my letter; for when I think of her misfortunes, I may say with Edgar, "O fortune! . . . (Stev, p. 289)

When Hetty saw her mother, Mary does not say. The visit was about a month before the birth of her first child.

However, soon some of the members of the family began to take a different attitude toward Hetty and the entire episode. In 1725, Samuel Wesley, Jr. had visited his parents, who at the time were living at Wroot. His visit was probably shortly before May 10th. His father wrote to John on that day stating, "Your brother Samuel (with his wife) and Charles, are here."(JWL, I, p. 161) Samuel may have been trying not only to straighten out the family finances — he had lent money to his father — but also to ascertain all the facts about Hetty. Samuel, Jr. was sincerely and honestly disturbed. Living in Westminster, he might well have evaded the entire affair. But he felt an allegiance to his family and to his conscience to do what he could to rectify matters. He apparently was unsuccessful, but his concern continued.

John also felt that the family, particularly his father, had been unnecessarily hard upon Hetty. When he was home during the Summer of 1726 — a year after Samuel, Jr's. attempt to reconcile the family differences — John spoke again and again with his father on Hetty's behalf. He made no impression on the stubborn old man. On August 28th he preached from his father's pulpit at Wroot on "Universal Charity" or "Charity Due to Wicked Persons."

Both Samuel Sr. and Susanna were deeply hurt. Samuel spoke to Charles about what John had done "Every day you hear how he contradicts me and takes your sister's part before my face; nay, he disputes with me, preaches . . ." (JWL, I, pp. 202, 203) and his voice trailed off into silence.

Charles reported the conversation to John, who immediately sought reconciliation with his father. They wept together and his father told John that he always knew John was good at heart. John promised to help his father with his work on Job, which he did the next day; and both men, for a time, seemed to forget about poor Hetty.

However, Samual still rankled under the lash of his son's sermon. He apparently wrote to Samuel, Jr., who, in turn, inquired of John exactly what took place. Samuel, Sr. had gone so far as to say that John in his sermon had violated the 53rd Canon of the Church. The Canon has to do with a preacher proclaiming a doctrine in contradiction to that preached by a colleague in such a way as to cause trouble in the congregation. In such a case, the matter was to be immediately reported to the bishop. No one, of course, reported John's sermon to the bishop. His mother, Susanna, however, took John to task for his sermon and charged him with preaching the entire sermon for the last paragraphs, which were meant to defend Hetty against the family's attitude. Susanna, of course, was right. John made this clear in a letter to his brother:

> My sister Hetty's behaviour has, for ought I have heard, been innocent enough since her marriage. Most of my disputes on charity with my father were on her account, he being inconceivably exasperated against her. 'Tis likely enough he would not see her when at Wroote; he has disowned her long ago, and never spoke of her in my hearing but with the utmost detestation. Both he, my mother, and several of my sisters were persuaded her pentience was but feigned. One great reason for my writing the above mentioned sermon was to endeavor, as far as in me lay, to convince them that even on supposition that she was impenitent some tenderness was due to her still; which my mother when I read it to her was so well aware of that she told me as soon as I had read it, "You writ this sermon for Hetty; the rest was brought in for the sake of the last paragraph." (JWL, I, p. 205)

A curious incident occurred in the Fall of 1726, following John Wesley's attempt at reconciling his parents with Hetty. Susanna, herself, wrote to John on October 12th that the Wrights (Hetty and her husband) were even then visiting the Lamberts, Hetty's sister Anne and her husband. Anne, or "Nancy" Wesley had married Lambert, a land surveyor, on December 2, 1725 (see Chapter Six) and evidently a friendship had sprung up between the Wrights and the Lamberts that lasted throughout their lives. Lambert and Wright may have been friends before Wright's marriage to Hetty. Why or when Anne had softened her attitude toward Hetty is not known. John's sermon may have greatly influenced all the family. But more to the point is the fact that, apparently with her husband's consent, Susanna went to see Hetty at the Lambert's home. Her discussion with Hetty, however, was unsatisfactory. The letter to John describing the meeting is written by Susanna and from Susanna's viewpoint, and is difficult to interpret.

Certainly it reveals that Hetty's mother was in a state of extreme conflict for a person of her usual composure. She pictures Hetty as completely indifferent to her advances. She writes that she herself spoke what she thought proper for the occasion. Then she added, "I told her I freely forgave her all her offenses against me, and spoke more perhaps than was required on my part." (JWL, I, p. 199F) Susanna proposed a meeting between Hetty and her father, but Hetty apparently feared the confrontation, stating that her father would only reproach her with what was past. Susanna stoutly defended her husband and stated that he would certainly put Hetty in mind of her faults as was his duty as a parent and a pastor.

This was hardly the most charitable approach to a person who had already admitted her faults and entered into a disastrous marriage to please her parents. The whole conversation was unsatisfactory and Susanna returned home "Neither pleased with her or myself."

Then, strangely enough, she added, "I desire what I've spoken of Hetty may be concealed. I have not spoken so freely of her to our folks nor is it necessary that they shall know my thoughts. Let all think as they please." She does not say whether she reported her conversation with Hetty to her husband; probably she said little.

Unfortunately, Susanna's offer of forgiveness was neither generous nor well expressed. Hetty had committed no offense against her mother. She was well on into her twenties when she went to London with the man who had deceived her. She had later acquiesed to a marriage forced on her by her parents and was trying to make the best of it. She had received no support or help, spiritual or otherwise from her parents. She was in reality more sinned against than sinning.

Susanna probably sensed all this, but with her eighteenth century background and her respect for her husband whom she defended whenever necessary, she was in a state of uncertainty and conflict, which eventually took its toll on her health. She had a strong sense of what was fitting and proper, but she lacked that warm spirit of love that would have prompted her to have taken Hetty into her arms and in spite of her husband's attitude to have restored her to the family circle.

The situation now was becoming increasingly painful. December 10th, 1726 Samuel, Jr. wrote to his brother John, "I wish my mother and sister Emily were heartily reconciled to Hetty. I am resolved to do what I can do both with them and my father." (JWL, I, p. 207) He recognized the uncharitable attitude of his parents and some of his sisters, but he did not condemn them. In Samuel's mind their action was based on the assumption that Hetty was not truly repentant. If this were the case, he wanted it clearly understood that he agreed with them, and so he added in his note to John "though upon supposition indeed of her being penitent, otherwise I will never plead for innocence and guilt's being treated alike." Samuel, Jr. could empathize with both Hetty and the other members of the family. He understood them well.

Probably late in 1726, Hetty and her husband moved to London. Here, with the help of the five hundred pounds her Uncle Matthew had given Hetty as a wedding present, Wright set up his own shop in Crown Court, Dean's Street near Soho. Charles Wesley visited the Wrights and in a letter to his brother dated January 20th, 1727, he wrote:

> 'Tis but a week before I left London that I knew she was at it [London]. Little of that time you may be sure did I lose, being with her almost constantly; I could almost envy myself the doat of pleasure I had crowded in that small space. In a little neat room she has hired did the good natured, ingenuous, contented creature watch, and I talk over a few short days, which we both wished had been longer. As yet, she lives pretty well, having but herself and honest W. Wright to keep, though I fancy there's another a-coming. Brother Samuel and Sister are very kind to her, and I hope will continue so, for I have cautioned her never to contradict my sister, whom she knows. . . . My sister Wright begs you to write to her, at Wakeden's, in Crown Court, Dean's Street, near Soho Square. (Stev, p. 304)

Charles was right in his conjecture about Hetty's physical condition. She was again pregnant, and she returned to Louth to her husband's parents to have her baby. Here she was surprised to receive a visit from her father. Martha reported the visit in a letter to her brother John:

> My father has been at Louth to see sister Wright, who by good providence was brought to bed two days before he got thither, which perhaps might prevent his saying what he otherwise might have said to her; for none that deserves the name of a man would say anything to grieve a woman in a condition where grief is often present death to them.
>
> I fancy that you have heard before now that my brother Willy is gone off for debt, he having been bound for his father, and that sister Hetty's child is dead. (Stev, p. 362)

The amount of tragedy packed into these few sentences is staggering. The presence of an irate, tactless, cruel father; a woman in childbirth—lonely and afraid—her husband in jail for his own father's debts, and finally a dead baby, the second to die since its mother's marriage.

We do not know when or how Wright managed to pay off his father's debts and return from a debtor's prison to his own shop. Possibly Hetty, herself, aided her husband through work as a teacher. Samuel, her brother, in a letter to John, written about may of 1727, stated:

> I have received a letter from my sister Hetty since my last to you, wherein she tells me her child is dead, and she has set up a school; by which, though not meeting with so much encouragement as she expected, she hopes to get food at least, and somewhat to put her out of her present condition of a heathen philosopher. (JWL, I, pp. 219, 220)

All the Wesley sisters had received sufficient training from their parents to act as teachers or governesses; but we have no way of knowing how successful Hetty's school proved to be or how long it lasted or even how many pupils she may have gathered. What is important to Hetty, however, was that she was slowly being received back into the family circle.

Charles and John had joined with Mary in accepting Hetty into a full relationship with themselves. Hetty and her husband were friends of John Lambert, who was married to Anne, Hetty's sister, and the two couples apparently visited each other frequently. Samuel, Jr. and his wife were proving to be good friends to Hetty, although, in the main, Samuel tended to place himself in a neutral position as a negotiator who refuses to take sides, in the hope thereby of having greater influence in reconciling both parties.

Shipwreck

In the meantime Wright's conduct toward his wife became more and more atrocious. He spent a large portion of his time in near-by taverns, coming home late and often drunk. He began to neglect his business and to abuse his wife physically.

Hetty, in her despair, wrote a long poem to her husband which he may not have understood, even if he ever had taken the trouble to read it. Under the circumstances, it is a moving poem; and although not great poetry, it has some excellent lines:

> The ardent lover cannot find
> A coldness in his fair unkind,
> But blaming what he cannot hate,
> He mildly chides the dear ingrate,
> And though despairing of relief,
> In soft complaining vents his grief.
> Then what should hinder but that I,

Impatient of my wrongs, may try,
By saddest softest strains, to move
My wedded, latest, dearest love,
To throw his cold neglect aside,
And cheer once more his injured bride?
   O thou, whom sacred rites designed
My guide, and husband ever kind,
My sovereign master, best of friends,
On whom my earthly bliss depends;
If e'er thou didst in Hetty see
Aught fair, or good, or dear to thee,
If gentle speech can ever move
The cold remains of former love,
Turn thee at last—my bosom ease,
Or tell me why I cease to please.
   Is it because revolving years,
Heart-breaking sighs, and fruitless tears,
Have quite deprived this form of mine
Of all that once thou fanciedst fine?
Ah no! what once allured thy sight
Is still in its meridian height.
These eyes their usual lustre show
When uneclipsed by flowing woe.
Old age and wrinkles in this face
As yet could never find a place:
A youthful grace informs these lines,
Where still the purple current shines,
Unless, by thy ungentle art,
It flies to aid my wretched heart:
Nor does this slighted bosom show
The thousand hours it spends in woe.
   Or is it that, oppressed with care,
I stun with loud complaints thine ear;
And make thy home for quiet meant
The seat of noise and discontent?
Ah no! those ears were ever free
From matrimonial melody:
For though thine absence I lament
When half the lonely night is spent,
Yet when the watch or early morn
Has brought me hopes of thy return,
I oft have wiped these watchful eyes,
Concealed my cares, and curbed my sighs,
In spite of grief, to let thee see
I wore an endless smile for thee.
  Had I not practised every art
T'oblige, divert, and cheer thy heart,
To make me pleasing in thine eyes,
And turn thy house to paradise;
I had not asked, "Why dost thou shun
These faithful arms, and eager run

To some obscure, unclean retreat,
With fiends incarnate glad to meet,
The vile companions of thy mirth,
The scum and refuse of the earth;
Who, when inspired by beer, can grin
At witless oaths and jests obscene,
Till the most learned of the throng
Begins a tale of ten hours long;
While thou, in raptures, with stretched jaws
Crownest each joke with loud applause?"
    Deprived of freedom, health, and ease,
And rivalled by such things as these;
This latest effort will I try,
Or to regain thy heart, or die.
Soft as I am, I'll make thee see
I will not brook contempt from thee!
    Then quit the shuffling doubtful sense,
Nor hold me longer in suspense;
Unkind, ungrateful, as thou art,
Say, must I ne'er regain thy heart?
Must all attempts to please thee prove
Unable to regain thy love?
    If so, by truth itself I swear,
The sad reverse I cannot bear:
No rest, no pleasure, will I see;
My whole of bliss is lost with thee!
I'll give all thoughts of patience o'er;
(A gift I never lost before);
Indulge at once my rage and grief,
Mourn obstinate, disdain relief,
And call that wretch my mortal foe,
Who tries to mitigate my woe;
Till life, on terms severe as these,
Shall, ebbing, leave my heart at ease,
To thee thy liberty restore
To laugh when Hetty is no more. (Stev. p. 307)

Her effort was totally ineffective. Wright continued to go his own way.

Their trouble stemmed partly from their intellectual and social differences. These differences are sharply etched in a letter written by Wright to John Wesley announcing the birth and death of Hetty's third child. He explains that their baby died three days after birth, but that his wife is doing well. Then Wright adds a postscript:

Ive sen you Sum verses that my wife maid of Dear Lamb. Let me hear from one or both of you as soon as you think conveniant. (Harmon, p. 129)

The verses had been dictated to her husband by Hetty and first appeared in Wright's interesting form of spelling. Entitled *A Mother's Address to Her*

Dying Infant, they appeared later in a corrected version in *The Arminian Magazine.* The letter and the verses reveal that there must have been a warm, good-hearted streak in Wright; but they also reveal that Wright was out of his depth both intellectually and socially in the Wesley family.

Adding to Hetty's sorrow at the deaths of her babies was her father's continuing wrath. She became somewhat hysterical in her search for his forgiveness, imagining that God's anger was directed toward her because of her father's refusal to forgive her or intercede for her. In an undated letter she wrote:

> Should God give and take away another (child), I can never escape the thought that my father's intercession might have prevailed against His wrath, which I shall then take to be also manifest. Forgive me, sir . . . But as you planted my matrimonial bliss so you cannot run away from my prayer when I beseech you to water it with a little kindness. My brothers will report to you what they have seen of my way of life and my daily struggle to redeem the past. But I have come to a point where I feel your forgiveness to be necessary to me. I beseech you then not to withold it. (Harmon, p. 131 ff)

Samuel's caustic reply to this piteous appeal demonstrates how deeply hurt and resentful he must have felt with the conduct of his favorite daughter.

In a more rational moment Hetty insisted that the deaths of her children were occasioned by the lead fumes from her husband's plumbing shop. She was probably right. In this she proved herself to be a sound early environmentalist. The infant mortality rate in 18th century England was exceedingly high regardless of the natural surroundings; but lead fumes would not help to preserve the life of a newborn infant.

The Better Life

Hetty's life with its frustrations, sorrows, disappointments and despair had periods of brightness. She was now in touch with both Charles and John, and her brother Samuel aided her as much as his income permitted. Her Uncle Matthew continued to take a special interest in her. He appreciated her mental endowments, her physical beauty and her kindly nature. On one occasion he invited her to accompany him on a trip to Bath and Tunbridge, and she visited him occasionally at his home. Here she met people of the literary world and others in keeping with the social standing of the Wesleys. Since Wright, himself, does not seem to have accompanied her on any of these occasions, it may have caused a deepening of the breech between them. Wright, of course, would have felt uncomfortable with a class of people with whom Hetty moved at ease.

In addition, Hetty's poetical works were later to appear in various magazines: *The Gentleman's Magazine, The Poetical Register, The Christian Magazine,,* and *The Arminian Magazine.* Some of her poems were sent to immediate members of the family and were subsequently lost. However, it might be well to note that a truly fine work, *Eupolis His Hymn to the Creator,* which has always been ascribed to her father, Samuel Wesley, Sr., may have been written in part at least by Hetty herself. Researchers have discovered that a large part of this poem had been written in Hetty's handwriting, with editing in Samuel's. This is by no means conclusive evidence, since Hetty acted at times as her father's amanuensis, but it is suggestive that she may have had more to do with this poem than has been credited to her.

At least her talent was greatly appreciated by a small group of friends. A gentleman signing himself *Silvius* wrote two poems for *The Gentleman's Magazine,* in which he lauded Hetty's poetry and suggested that she publish a volume of her own verses. Hetty apparently never considered the possibility, but the suggestion must have brought her great satisfaction. The opening lines contain the poet's description of Hetty, which reveals her as a woman of great beauty in spite of her numerous troubles. The name *Granvilla* in the opening lines, of course, refers to Hetty, herself. The work is entitled *To Mrs. W   T, On Reading Her Manuscript Poems*:

> Fain would my grateful muse a trophy raise
> Devoted to Granvilla's lasting praise.
> But from what topic shall her task begin?
> From outward charms, or richer stores within?
> 'Twere difficult with portrait just to trace
> The blooming beauties of her lovely face;
> The roseate bloom that blushes on her cheek;
> Her eyes, whence rays of pointed lightning break;
> Each brow the bow of Cupid, whence her darts
> With certain archery strike unguarded hearts;
> Her lips, that with a rubied tincture glow,
> Soft as the soothing sounds which from them flow.
> But Oh! what words, what numbers shall I find
> T'express the boundless treasures of her mind,
> Where wit and judgment spread their copious mines,
> And every grace and every virtue shines! (Stev. p. 312)
> . . .

The writer continues in this florid, exaggerated style, but he certainly seems sincere in his appreciation of Hetty's mind and beauty. It is doubtful if Wright was aware of Hetty's triumphs. Had he been, he probably would have put a stop to Hetty's visits to her uncle and her friends. For a time he refused to allow her to attend any meetings of the Methodists.

Last Days in The Search For Love

Hetty grew closer and closer to her Uncle Matthew. She appreciated his tolerant, Christian spirit, and he enjoyed her company, her brilliant mind, and her compassionate, understanding attitude towards life. On more than one occasion he had become desperately ill, and Hetty nursed him back to health. He finally died in her arms in 1737, one year before John Wesley's Aldersgate experience. In his will he left Hetty two hundred pounds, and to Amelia Wright, his great niece, a hundred pounds. This would indicate that at least one of Hetty's children lived beyond infancy, but there is no extant record that the girl reached maturity. She may even have been dead by the time Matthew's will was read.

Three years before this event Mary Whitelamb, Hetty's sister had died. Hetty never forgot Mary's love and care for her during the time of her mental and spiritual suffering.

Hetty's father had died at Epworth April 25th, 1735. There is no record that Hetty was present on this occasion. Mrs. Harmon is probably right when she states, "He would not have wanted her there!" (Harmon, p. 135) He had never sought her company nor forgiven her so-called sin. He had visited her once at Louth when she was about to have her second child, but only her physical condition had prevented him from speaking the cruel, vicious words that seemed to gush naturally from his lips whenever he thought of her.

He had often stated that through his prayers God had given him the certainty that all his children would be with him in eternity — a statement that is difficult to understand in the light of his attitude toward the most brilliant of his daughters.

After her father's death, life became a little easier for Hetty. Her husband seemed to soften in his attitude toward her. She, in turn, more and more sought for company among her Methodist friends. Eventually she became a Methodist.

Her mother, Susanna, also after her husband's death went through a change. For a time she lived with Emily at Gainsborough, but she eventually took up permanent residence in The Foundery, a building John Wesley had established in London for a meeting house, a preachers' house, and an apartment for his mother and his sister, Emily, together with one of Emily's servants. During these years Hetty and her mother were reconciled, suggesting that had it not been for Samuel, Susanna would long since have restored Hetty to her affections.

It remains a puzzle why Susanna did not withstand her husband and champion the cause of Hetty. Some biographers think she was in a state of constant conflict between her desire to forgive Hetty and restore her to the family circle, and her sense of duty to obey Samuel's stern commands. She was torn, writes Mrs. Harmon, "between her love for her daughter" and what has been called her "conscientious refusal to countenance her." Mrs. Harmon goes so far as to suggest that the inner conflict almost caused her death at an earlier period in her life. (Harmon, p. 135)

Time healed the rift in the Wesley family. With Samuel dead, and with all his surviving daughters living in and around London, the former happy fellowship was resumed and Hetty was part of the new life. When Susanna finally died in 1742, all her surviving daughters were present, as was John.

After her mother's death, however, Hetty's health notably declined. She had had a difficult life. She had borne a number of children, had courageously faced an unhappy marriage which she tried in every possible way to salvage, and now she was tired. She became an invalid, her health broken. To the credit of her husband, Wright, he seems to have tried to care for her in his own crude way. At least he remained with her.

Her strength and peace however, now came through a new found faith in God. In a remarkable letter to her brother John she writes:

> I have long desired to know one thing, Jesus Christ and Him crucified, and this desire prevails above all others. . . . I am enabled to seek Him still, and to be satisfied with nothing else than God. . . . (Stev, p. 315)

Her brothers tried to help restore her health by sending her to a health spa at Bristol. The Methodists of this predominantly Methodist city surrounded her with friendship and love, but her health was little improved.

While she was at Bristol she wrote a lengthy letter to her brother John. Her husband Wright had remained in London and in her letter she demonstrates her concern for his welfare. She asks her brother not to forget him and adds, "I should rejoice had you any hope of him or that any outward sin was struck off."

She wishes that John might come to Bristol for the church there needs him badly. She makes light of her own illness and lauds many of the Methodists who were trying to make her stay a pleasant one.

However, even after all the years since her first miss-step, she still feels the weight of condemnation — some of it apparently directed at her by other Methodists. She writes:

> My brother Charles advises me to go into the bands, which I would willingly, if I thought I should not bring still more disgrace upon you, by being turned out again, having everything to fear from myself.

It would seem apparent that some Methodists still recalled the scandal connected with her name, and had made her feel unwelcome. On the other hand, she may have been oversensitive, for she mentions by name many of the Bristol Methodists who "load me with obligations." (JWL, II, p. 112)

When she returned to London, she was confined to bed. Charles often visited her, and on one occasion she said to him, "I have long ardently wished for death, because, you know, we Methodists always die in a transport of joy." (Stev, p. 317)

But even this consolation was denied her. She died with doubts and suffering. By a curious coincidence her life came to an end on March 21st, 1750, while London was in a state of fear and unrest due to a series of earthquakes that spread great alarm throughout the city. Her death seems to have been as storm ridden as her life.

Charles recorded her last days in his Journal. On Monday, March 5th, 1750, he wrote: "I prayed by my sister Wright, a gracious, tender, trembling soul; a bruised reed which the Lord will not break." On Wednesday, March 14th he wrote, "I found my sister Wright very near the haven; and again on Sunday the 18th, yet still in darkness, doubts and fears against hope believing in hope." (CWJ, II, pp. 68, 69)

She died March 21st. Only Charles of the Wesley family was at her burial place, which today is unknown. Her lonely, fear-filled end was characteristic of her lifetime search for love which had led her to some of the most disastrous experiences of any of the seven Wesley sisters.

Her husband Wright, according to Charles Wesley, was inconsolable at her death. As he had grown older he had grown more mellow, and was less cruel to his wife. He allowed his wife greater liberties, as we have seen, and he apparently took a greater interest in his own business. He continued his friendship with the Lamberts, and was a drinking companion of John Lambert, much to the sorrow of Charles Wesley. He stood by his wife in her illness and permitted her to take advantage of the ministrations of her Uncle and later her brothers. Fundamentally he was a good-hearted person. His life, also, had its tragic aspects. He was out of his depth both socially and intellectually among the Wesleys and their friends, and he was keenly aware of his shortcomings. His life was certainly not a happy one.

Following the death of Hetty, Martha, her sister, came to live with Wright for a time as a kind of housekeeper. The arrangement did not last very long; Wright soon married again, and his connection with the Wesley family was broken.

However, he apparently sent for Charles Wesley when he was dying. George J. Stevenson records an undated letter of Charles Wesley in which he speaks of Wright's final hours:

> He is struck down by the dead-palsy; longed above all things for my coming; rejoiced and wept to see me. His stubborn heart was much softened by the approach of death. Now he is a poor sinner indeed, full of horror and self-condemnation, yet not without hope of mercy. I prayed again with my poor pentitent, and left him a little more easy and composed. Shortly after, a messenger called me, between one and two, to my brother. He told me he was dying; that his feet were dead already; he was perfectly sensible; told me before his wife how he had settled his affairs, not enough to her advantage, I think; expressed a hope and earnest desire for one, one only thing—for the voice of a trumpet to warn all mankind not to walk in the paths wherein he had walked; made me witness to his reconciliation with his wife; and said he expected to die at four or five. I spoke comfortably to him of Jesus, our Atonement, our Peace, our Hope; prayed with much freedom, as we did last night in the Society; saw no symptoms of immediate death, yet could not lessen his apprehension of it. . . . (Stev, p. 320)

Wright died shortly after Charles Wesley returned to his Society meeting to preach.

EPILOGUE

No one has ever gathered together the poems of Hetty Wesley. Adam Clarke in his volume on *Memoirs of the Wesley Family* printed those which I assume, he thought were among her best. Many of her poems were sent to members of her family and subsequently lost. Others appeared in different household magazines and *The Gentleman's Magazine.* The sad strain that is evident throughout her poetry would probably make them morbid reading, and for that reason unacceptable to the public. However, the beauty of some of her lines is worth preserving, and make the reading of her poetry a rewarding experience. The opening four lines of her verse, *A Mother's Address to Her Dying Infant* might well have been written by William Blake:

> Tender softness! infant mild!
> Perfect, purest, brightest child!
> Transient lustre! Beauteous clay!
> Smiling wonder of a day!

Chapter Six

As a Quiet Stream
The Story of Anne Wesley
Mrs. John Lambert

We know little about Anne Wesley. What we do know would indicate that her life moved forward as a quiet stream, and that she found the love for which five of her sisters sought in vain.

There were no dramatic episodes in Anne's biography; but she enjoyed a quality of life which brought her deep satisfaction. There was a mutual love and affection between her and her husband out of which grew a spirit of quiet contentment. Anne was always in touch with her brothers and sisters. She nursed John through a brief illness in London and, along with her four sisters, she was at the deathbed of her mother. For the most part, however, she enjoyed her husband and her home.

Childhood

Anne, together with her twin brother John Benjamin, was born at Epworth May 17, 1701. They were both baptised on May 31st of that year. Seven months thereafter her brother died. About this time also Anne's mother, Susanna, began that strict schooling of her children which made the Wesley sisters among the best educated women of their day.

When Anne was five years old her mother taught her the letters of the alphabet in a day-and-a-half. Since all her other children, with the exception of Mary, had learned their letters in a day, her mother thought Anne was rather dull. By this time, Samuel, her brother, was at Westminster School in London, and Anne and her sisters comprised Susanna's entire class. All the sisters progressed rapidly. In addition Anne probably joined the recreational activities of her family and seemed to enjoy playing cards and dancing. At least, later in life, after her marriage, she invited friends and relatives on numerous occasions to *quadrilles* and possibly cards.

In 1709 she was saved from the rectory fire by her father who first looked to the safety of some of his children, and then began searching for his wife. The entire family was saved before the building collapsed.

Anne was in her teens when the rectory was haunted by "Old Jeffrey." Her account gives us an unusual picture of her character and courage.

Her father was convinced that the ghost, or whatever it was that haunted the Wesley household, could be frightened away by noise. One night, hearing ghostly noises, he sent Anne, then only sixteen years old, into the garret to blow loudly on a horn. As she faced the steps leading to the dark attic, the noises could be clearly heard. Anne was terrorized. She offered a short prayer. She prayed that since what she was doing was not of her own will but that of another, she hoped the ghost would take no offense and would do her no harm.

The brave little teen-ager then ascended the steps to the garret. As she entered the room to blow the horn, the noises ceased. However, they began again later, louder than ever. Evidently, the blowing of the horn had little effect, other than to arouse the entire household.

On another occasion, while she was sitting on the side of her bed playing cards with her sisters, the bed began to rise. Anne jumped off. When the bed returned to the floor, she was persuaded again to sit on the bed only to have it rise to a greater height. She jumped off once more, but could not be persuaded again to resume her former place. She feared "Old Jeffrey" might be trying to carry her away.

In addition, Jeffrey seemed to follow her about more than any other member of the family. When she crossed a room, his footsteps could be heard following hers. Whatever she did, he mimicked. However, with the usual Wesley pragmatism, she soon became accustomed to these antics and scornfully ignored them.

The little we know about Anne comes from the letters of her parents, her brothers and sisters, and the Journals of John and Charles Wesley. John corresponded with her fairly regularly, but the entire correspondence seems to have been lost. She was nicknamed "Nancy," a common designation for Anne in eighteenth century England. She worked for a time as a governess or companion in a family at Thorne, but returned home when her mistress became ill.

John Lambert and Marriage

On September 10th, 1724, Martha Wesley wrote to her brother John, "Sister Nancy, I believe, will marry John Lambert: perhaps you may not have forgotten him since you saw him at Wroote." (Stev, p. 358)

John Lambert was a land surveyor and an important figure at Epworth. A highly intelligent person, he had received a good education, was prosperous in his business, and enjoyed reading. Soon after meeting Samuel Wesley, Sr., he began collecting the writings of the rector, making notes in the margins of some of the publications. He is credited by George Stevenson, an important nineteenth century biographer of the Wesleys, with rescuing some of the tracts of Samuel Wesley which might otherwise have completely disappeared. The collection was used by Adam Clarke, an earlier biographer, in his book on *Memoirs of the Wesley Family*.

John Wesley had evidently met Lambert on the occasion of one of Lambert's visits to the Wesleys or while he was courting Anne. Fortunately, Lambert did not seem to have made much of an impression on John, who, as a result, found little to criticize. Had he known that Lambert was mildly addicted to alcohol, he might have objected to the courtship. It would have been a serious mistake had any of the Wesleys interfered with the marriage, since Lambert was a man of wealth and importance in the community, and an ideal match for Anne. They were married at Finningly December 2nd, 1725.

Mrs. Wesley provided Anne with a liberal dowry, for which the Wesleys went into debt. Their resources were smaller than usual because of a disastrous storm that ruined their crops at Wroot. After the wedding the Lamberts went to live near the church in a little red house which Mrs. Wesley said they had made very pretty and comfortable.

Samuel Wesley, Jr. was so pleased with the marriage that he wrote a poem of eleven quatrains *To My Sister Lambert on Her Marriage*. The last three stanzas of the poem reveal the strong male chauvinistic attitude common in eighteenth century England.

> Firm let the husband's empire stand,
>   With easy but unquestioned sway;
> May he have kindness to command,
>   And thou the bravery to obey!
>
> Long may he give thee comfort, long
>   As the frail knot of life shall hold!
> More than a father when thou'rt young,
>   More than a son when waxing old.
>
> The greatest earthly pleasure try.
>   Allowed by Providence Divine;
> Be he a husband blest as I.
>   And thou a wife as good as mine!
>   (Stev, p. 324)

The couple seem to have been happy from the first day of their marriage. John Wesley especially enjoyed visiting his sister and her husband, and frequently wrote to her.

In his diary under the date of May 16th, 1726, he notes that it is "my sister Nancy's birthday" and four days later he records a visit to her home. (JWJ, Vol. I, p. 70)

On December 6th, 1726, in a letter to his brother Samuel, he mentions that he dined "at my sister Lambert's and was her son's godfather." He adds, "I was detained there by fresh company coming in till evening." In his diary he notes another fact. "Danced!" (JWL, I, p. 203) Apparently on the occasion of the baptism of her son, who was named John after his father, Anne invited a great many friends into her home for dancing and possibly cards. There may also have been a certain amount of drinking. Everyone seemed to have had a happy time, and John records no criticism of the affair in his diary.

Later in John's letter to Samuel he notes that Samuel is displeased with the Lamberts for some reason, possibly because of their penchant for parties. John sweeps aside the criticism and adds, "My sister Lambert behaved herself unexceptionably while we were in the country; that she had lately altered her conduct, which indeed is highly improbable, I did not hear till now." (JWL, I, p. 205)

In his reply Samuel defended himself and his sister Anne. He wrote:

> You are widely mistaken if you think I charge sister Lambert with an alteration for the worse in her conduct. I suppose the very contrary, and therefore, wonder there should be any alteration for the worse in her treatment from others — if any such there be. (JWL, I, p. 207)

It is an obscure reference difficult to interpret. Sometime later, however, both brothers seem a little vexed with Lambert who evidently tried to borrow money from John. On May 15, 1727 Samuel wrote:

> Brother Lambert may want money perhaps sufficiently, but I am sure he does not want confidence to ask you to lend it to him; I am afraid that you have more than one reason for not complying with so unreasonable a request. (JWL, I, p. 220)

Evidently the Lamberts had been fairly well off, and this request for a loan can be interpreted either as a sign of mismanagement or possibly a desire on the part of Lambert to expand his business. His cash flow also may have been reduced due possibly to his partying or drinking. It is difficult to say. Whatever the reason, he was unsuccessful in moving any of the Wesleys to assist him. Since the brothers were always ready to help their relatives, especially when they were in need, the reference probably suggests Lambert's desire to expand his business, something the Wesleys were not about to aid. They were ready to help but not to invest. Nor would they have assisted Lambert if his need for a loan arose from his and Anne's style of living.

Whatever the reason for Samuel's comment, it evidently had nothing to do with any difficulty between Anne and her husband. They were as happy as birds, especially in the progress of their son, John.

The boy survived his infancy, always a critical time in eighteenth-century England with its high infant mortality rate. How much longer he lived, we do not know. He was probably still living when Anne's Uncle Matthew died, since Matthew bequeathed one hundred pounds to "my nephew, John Lambert." (Stev, pp. 52, 53) The boy would have been about nine years of age.

In addition, by the fall of 1726, Anne had apparently reached out a hand of forgiveness and love to her sister Hetty, who was still a source of disgrace in her father's mind (see Chapter Five). Apparently John Lambert must have known William Wright, Hetty's husband, before he married into the Wesley family. The two men, it would seem, had little in common save a liking for liquor and the sociability of the local taverns. For a time Wright was a traveling plumber, and, in his capacity as a land surveyor, Lambert also did a great deal of traveling. The two men may have met quite frequently. But whatever drew the men together the Wrights visited the Lamberts, who always opened their house to guests. Anne had no reason for witholding her affection from Hetty, and Hetty was only too happy to renew her relationship with any member of the family. When, therefore, the Lamberts invited the Wrights to their home for a visit, the Wrights gladly responded. Here, as we have seen, Hetty met with her mother, Susanna, in an unsatisfactory interview (See Chapter Five). We would probably know little or nothing of the event had not Susanna written about it to her son John, who preserved her letter. The Lamberts and the Wrights became lifelong friends, and the husbands were often seen together.

John Wesley's early friendship with the Lamberts did not go unnoticed, especially by other members of the Wesley family. John's sister Martha, in a letter dated February 17, 1727, notes that John had recently written to Anne and had sent her a package, but had not written to Martha, which hurt her deeply. Later in the letter she adds,

> I have read the plays you sent sister Lambert several times, for 'tis a great pleasure to me to read a good play, though I have the same fate in that as in most other things I like, I have them very seldom. (Stev, p. 325)

The plays may have been part of the package which John had sent to the Lamberts.

Nevertheless, for a while, the Lamberts must have fallen on hard times financially. Possibly Lambert's attempts to expand his business were unsuccessful, or possibly his work simply dried up. His occupation may have been seasonable, and without good management, his cash flow might well have been cut off. It is difficult to say. At any rate in a letter to John written by his mother on August 11, 1729, Susanna stated:

> I need not tell you I should be glad to see you, because you know it already; and so I should to see poor Charles too; but what to say to his coming I know not. John Lambert, his wife and child, we are still like to keep, for we hear no news of a place for him; though I would fain hope it would please God to provide for him in some say 'ere winter, and take off their weight which really grows very heavy. (JWL, I, p. 239)

Eventually, however, Lambert regained his financial status, and together with his wife and family, moved to London. Here he and his wife became more friendly with Anne's Uncle Matthew Wesley. Later they moved to Hatfield, where Charles Wesley visited them several times.

Charles evidently saw some things in the life of Lambert of which he did not approve—probably Lambert's love of liquor. Under the date of August 17, 1737 he noted in his Journal:

After spending some time at Hatfield, I set out with my brother Lambert for London. At Epping he went back full of good resolution. (CWJ, I, p. 73)

Probably Charles had convinced Lambert to give up drinking. John and Charles Wesley were not opposed to the use of wine or even small beer. One of John Wesley's last letters was to *The Custom House* requesting the release of two dozen bottles of French claret which had been seized at the White Swan. He was ready to pay whatever duty was required, but his request was denied. The brothers, however, were strongly set against spiritous liquors which Lambert and his brother-in-law Wright enjoyed. There is no record that Anne was particularly disturbed by her husband's drinking habits. He apparently treated her well, giving her respect, love, and a good home. Three months after Lambert made his resolutions under Charles' guidance, Wesley noted in his Journal:

At Mr. Hutton's this evening my brothers Lambert and Wright visited me. The latter has corrupted the former, after all the pains I have taken with him, and brought him back to drinking. I was full, yet could not speak; prayed for meekness, and then set before Wright the things he had done, in the devil's name, toward reconverting a soul to him. He left us abruptly. I encouraged poor J. Lambert to turn again unto God. (CWJ, I, p. 80)

This rather dark picture of Lambert was probably colored by Charles' Methodist mores. For Charles, even one or two drinks would have been inexcusable. It is doubtful that Lambert was a heavy drinker, although George Stevenson, an important nineteenth-century Wesleyan biographer says that drink was his besetting sin. Stevenson also quotes an undocumented source as saying, "John Lambert has little religion!" (Stev, p. 327)

All of these statements must be received in the light of what the Wesleys and the early Methodists thought was religion. They would probably have agreed with the paraphrase of a famous quotation:

When I speak of religion I speak of Biblical Christianity, and when I speak of Biblical Christianity I mean Protestant Christianity, and when I speak of Protestant Christianity I mean Methodism.

Many Methodists probably held this viewpoint, and Lambert's easy-going Anglicanism would have been thought of by the Wesleys as no religion at all.

Regardless of Charles Wesley's opinion of John Lambert, certain facts are evident from the extant records. Early in his career John Wesley enjoyed visiting in the home of the Lamberts, found it a place where he could rest and recuperate from his strenuous efforts, and he was especially fond of his sister, Anne.

It should also be noted that on July 19th, 1738 Charles Wesley returned to the home of Mr. Bray, after ministering successfully to a group of criminals condemned to death. At Bray's he met his sister, Anne, and her husband and noted:

> I found my brother and sister Lambert there, and preached to them the Gospel of forgiveness, which they received without opposition. (CWJ, I, p. 123)

Late in December 1741 John became ill at the Foundery in London. Anne was present and cared for him. He continued his activities, although he had a debilitating fever. On January first he consented to remain in bed, provided that anyone who wished to talk with him might be permitted to see him. Fifty or sixty persons came to see him, and John was afraid that Anne might be offended by some of the people who frequented the Foundery. When he asked her if she had been offended she replied, "Offended! I wish I could always be with you. I thought I was in Heaven!" (JWJ, Vol. 2, pp. 519, 520) In her quiet way Anne was probably a deeply religious person and her husband an acceptable churchman.

The last extant record of Anne Lambert is a notation that she was at her mother's bedside with her four sisters when her mother died at the Foundery July 1742. She attended the funeral of her mother in Bunhill Fields. She was then about forty years of age. Where or how she died; whether or not she outlived her husband; and what became of her son is not known. What seems evident is that Anne accomplished what few of the Wesleys achieved — a happy marriage.

Chapter Seven

Living and Forgiving
The Story of Martha Wesley
Mrs. Westley Hall

We probably know more about Martha Wesley than of any of the Wesley sisters. Although what we know of any of them is essentially fragmentary, our knowledge of Martha is based mostly on her brief Journal, her numerous revealing letters, and references to her in the letters and Journals of her brothers and in James Boswell's *Life of Samuel Johnson*, the great English lexicographer. She lived the longest of any of the sisters, dying in her eighty-fifth year.* Being a close friend and confidant of her niece, Sarah, daughter of her brother Charles, Martha was the last link between the Epworth Wesleys and their succeeding generations. She shared recollections of her own life with Sarah who, in turn, forwarded them to Adam Clarke, one of the first biographers of the Wesley family. At her death July 12, 1791, she was interred in the same vault as her brother John, who had died a few months earlier on March 2nd.

Childhood and Youth

The birthdate of Martha is not known, but it is generally thought she was born at Epworth in the Year 1706. She entered her mother's family school when she was five years old, learning her letters, as did most of her sisters, in one day. Her brother John, born three years before her, was also at this time one of Susanna's pupils.

It was the custom for Susanna Wesley to require each child to aid and assist the next younger student. John taught Martha to write, and for this reason her handwriting closely resembles his. Whether she in turn taught her brother Charles to write is not known.

She was affectionately called "Patty" by her family, and she was the favorite daughter of her mother. Her brother Charles later commented on this fact, expressing his "wonder that so wise a woman as his mother could give way to such partiality, or did not better conceal it." (Clarke, p. 511)

Patty defended both her mother and herself by saying, "What my sisters call partiality was what they might all have enjoyed if they had wished it, which was permission to sit in my mother's chambers, when disengaged, to listen to her conversation with others and to her remarks on things and books out of schoolhours." (Clarke, p. 510) Patty was the most serious of the Wesley children, and it is conceivable that she took a small chair and, with her mother's permission, sat primly by while her mother conversed with her guests and friends.

---

* *The Gentleman's Magazine* states, her eighty-fourth year, the date is uncertain.

Once when her mother had entered the nursery, she found everyone except Patty cavorting about the room in high glee. She said very quietly, "You will all be more serious one day!"

"Shall I be more serious?" inquired Patty.

"No!" said her mother shortly. It was difficult for even her mother to imagine a child more serious than Patty.

However, Patty had practically no sense of humor. Nevertheless, later in life, she had sufficient judgment and wit to engage the attention of Samuel Johnson. Also, on one occasion, she wrote a delightful letter to her brother Charles, in which she gently chafed him for not writing to her.

> I once knew a pretty sort of youth in Oxford called Mr. Charles Wesley. I should be glad to hear if he is in the land of the living. (Green, p. 237, N.3)

She, herself, in speaking of wit, said that she was the only one of the family who did not possess it; and Charles often said, "Sister Patty was always too wise to be witty." (Stev. p. 379) She also objected to the use of irony and satire that abounded in the eighteenth century; and she once told her brother Sameul, Jr. that ridicule never cured any vice.

Patty was also close to her brother John. Even when she was a baby, crying and unhappy sometimes during her numerous illnesses, she could be immediately soothed by his mere presence. As she matured, she strongly resembled him, and had she dressed in John's clothing, she could easily have passed for him (Clarke, p. 512).

During John Wesley's days at Oxford Martha enjoyed nothing better on his visits home, than to hear him read plays; and once when she was in London, they went together to see Congreve's popular comedy *The Old Bachelor.*

Later in life, it was she who arranged a meeting between her brother John and Samuel Johnson. They met at two o'clock one afternoon at Johnson's home for dinner. The dinner was not ready until three. Wesley had set aside two hours for his conversation with the learned man, and immediately after dinner he departed, much to Johnson's chagrin.

Patty defended her brother by saying, "Why Doctor, my brother has been with you two hours!"

To which Johnson replied, "Two hours, Madam! I could talk all day and all night too with your brother." (C&M, p. 526)

She was less than three years old at the time of the parsonage fire in 1709. Like all the Wesley children, except Emily, she was placed with a friend or relative until the rectory could be rebuilt. In what home she was placed is not known. She was ten years of age when "Old Jeffrey" began haunting the rebuilt house. She did not write about her experiences, and she is seldom mentioned in the accounts written by her sisters and parents. In 1720, when she was about fourteen years old, she went to London to stay with her Uncle Matthew. Susanna and Hetty had preceded her in this delightful environment, and she loved London well enough to remain with her uncle three years. Later, after a few years at home, she returned to her uncle's house for another extended stay of possibly six years. During this time she made frequent visits to Epworth and Wroot to see her parents. While in London she often attended divine services at St. Paul's Cathedral and at St. Dunstan's Church, Fleet Street. Occasionally she visited her brother Samuel at Westminster. She learned quickly what all the Wesleys learned, namely, never cross Samuel Wesley's wife. She had one dispute with Samuel's wife which she related in a letter to her brother John after which she wisely had as little to do with her as possible. She wrote:

> I go sometimes to Westminster, but I am afraid it will be impossible for me ever to make a *friend* of my sister. She fell upon me the last time I was there for "giving myself such an *air* as to drink water," though she told me "she did not expect that I should leave it." I told her that if she could convince me that there was any ill in it, I would, and thank her for telling me of it; but I desired her in the *first place* to tell me what she meant by the word *"air"*, which she did not choose to do, I believe for a very good reason; so our dispute ended. (Stev, p. 363)

Affairs of the Heart

On September 13th, 1735, Martha or Patty Wesley made the greatest mistake of her life by marrying Westley Hall, a pupil of her brother John and a member of the Oxford Holy Club. Prior to that event, however, she had had numerous suitors. Of these, Martha was most serious about John Romley who had previously courted her sister Hetty. Their father had sternly forbidden any marriage between Hetty and Romley; but about 1724 Romley began seriously courting Martha. Apparently he was still at the Charity School in Wroot and possibly serving as curate for Samuel Wesley. It was a curious situation which could only end in unhappiness, since Samuel Wesley, Sr. would certainly oppose the marriage.

Patty described what happened in a letter to her brother John dated March 7, 1725. It is clear from her narration that Romley had made a deep impression on her and that she was heartbroken when her father interfered once again in his daughters' lives—this time forbidding Romley from even coming to the rectory. Patty mentions an old song as the reason for the rector's attitude, but the reference is not clear. She wrote:

> Dear Brother Jack, — I had answered your very obliging letter long before now, only your particular inquiry into Romley's affair put me upon so melancholy a task that you cannot wonder that I so long deferred the performance. You know that my father forbade him his house upon account of the old song when you were at Wroote, since which time I have never seen Romley. He wrote me several times since, and

we held a secret correspondence together for a little time before I came to Kelstein. I desire you would not be inquisitive how the intrigue broke off; the bare mention of it is much, much more than I can bear. . . . (Stev, p. 358)

When Samuel Wesley broke up the affair between Romley and Patty he did what he had done after severing the relationship between Hetty and Romley. He packed her off to Kelstein and offered her services as a companion to Mrs. Grantham. Probably he felt some obligation to the Granthams because of their kindness to Hetty, who had left them without apparent cause. Also he may have believed that it would be good for Patty to be placed in a new environment with new interests after being almost forcibly separated from Romley.

The treatment was a little like that used by wealthy families in the eighteenth century when they were trying to break up an unsatisfactory match between a son and an unsuitable woman. "Send him off to the continent," they would say, "until his passion cools." Now Samuel was sending Patty to the Granthams.

According to Patty, the Granthams, themselves, were opposed to receiving her, although this may be an exaggeration. Hetty had proved to be an admirable governess and companion and there was no reason to believe Patty would be less so. Nevertheless, in a letter to John, Patty stated that the Granthams told her "they should never have desired my company only my father proffered me, and they did not well know how to refuse me." In their defense, the Granthams may have sensed that Patty was serving at Kelstein against her own will. She had, in fact, written to John that she would rather have gone to her grave than to Kelstein where the Granthams lived. Then she added, "I am in great measure careless of what becomes of me." (Stev, pp. 358, 359)

She was certainly in a sad state mentally, probably on account of the Romley affair, and she may not have been able satisfactorily to perform her duties or to be a cheerful companion to anyone. The Granthams finally gave her two months' notice, indicating that she should be gone by May Day.

Patty hated the thought of returning to Epworth or Wroot where her parents sometimes lived. She wrote to John that she would not go home again "were I reduced to beggary." She decided rather to try her fortune in London; and then, as if admitting how sorely her heart had been tried by her separation from Romley, she added, "I am resolved not to marry yet till I forget Romley or see him again." (Stev. p. 359) Neither of these alternatives would be possible at home.

However, she did not go to London that summer but returned to Wroot. She was only in her late teens, and although she preferred her Uncle's home in London, her parents forced her to return to them. Here she was indeed lonely for a variety of reasons.

In Kelstein she had been entertained by a number of suitors whom she refers to as "my lovers." True, she scoffed at them, speaking of them as "a set of mortals who universally own me the most unaccountable woman that ever they knew." She also stated, "I am condemned to constant solitude, and have not been out of the town once since I came into it." (Stev, p. 359) All this was probably an exaggeration, and it suggests that Charles may have been right when he referred to her, in her youth, as a "grumble-towel." (Stev, p. 363) But at least this state of affairs was better than life at Epworth or Wroot. By this time Emily was away teaching; Susanna was married, and Anne and Hetty were soon to be married; Mary was considerably older than Patty and was still considered "the family jest," and Patty and Kezzy had little in common. Indeed, there was little excitement or merriment at Epworth until John or Charles would return from time to time for a visit.

Like her other sisters, Martha dearly loved her brothers and particularly John. Realising, therefore, that one reason she could not go to London had to do with finances that were being used to pay necessary fees for John's fellowship and education, she was content. Her letter to him from Wroot in September 1725 speaks of her happiness that he may yet be a Fellow at Oxford. "I shall be exceeding glad if you get the Fellowship you stand for . . . I believe you very well deserve to be happy, and I sincerely wish you may be so both in this life and the next."

As for herself, she was deeply depressed:

> For my own particular I have long looked upon myself to be what the world calls ruined — that is I believe that there will never be any provision made for me, but when my father dies I shall have my choice of three things, starving, going to a common service, or marrying meanly, as my sisters have done; none of which I like, though I do think it possible for a woman to be happy with a man that is not a gentleman, for he whose mind is virtuous is alone of noble kind. Yet where a man has neither religion, birth, riches or good nature, I can't see what a woman can expect but misery. (Stev, p. 360)

Two years later Martha was still living at Wroot and her letters were filled with complaints. She expressed her jealousy of Sally Kirkham with whom Wesley was probably enamoured at the time. She was offended that he seemed to be writing to his other sisters more often than to Martha, and she went so far as to write playfully that she had contemplated some kind of revenge upon him until she remembered the quotation from Marcus:

> Thou best of brothers, and thou best of friends,
> Pardon a weak, distempered soul that swells
> With sudden gusts, and sinks as soon in calms.

Then she added:

> I believe that I need not tell you that when we love any person very well we desire to be loved by them in the same degree, and though I cannot

possibly be so vain as to think that I do for my own personal merits deserve more love than my sisters, yet can you blame me if I sometimes wish I had been so happy as to have had the first place in your heart? (Stev, p. 362)

Not long after this depressing letter Martha's outlook brightened considerably. Her letters take on a new note of excitement. There are two reasons for her reaction. A new curate has arrived at Epworth and two further suitors are on the horizon. The curate is only of passing interest, but he is a *new* interest. In her letter she stated:

My father has got a curate! John Lambert heard of him when he was surveying some miles off. He was a perfect stranger to my father, and my father to him. I can't tell you exactly what sort of a man he is, because I have not yet found him out, though he has been a fortnight with us; but by the best judgment I can make of him I shall be in no danger of running into one extreme you warned me of, liking him too well. Most of our town people fancy him to be like Mr. Pennington [a former curate?]; indeed he's not unlike him in shape, and at least as genteel; but you will cease to wonder I should not like him very well when I tell you he thinks as differently from you as light from darkness — or else he is one of those cunning gentlement that think fit to dissemble their own sentiments till they have tried those of others. (JWL, I, p. 243)

In spite of the fact that Patty assured John she would not make the same mistake she made before and "like the new curate too well" (probably a reference to Romley), she, nevertheless, seems to have had numerous conversations with him and to have picked up some of the village gossip concerning him. More than any other of her sisters, Martha needed male companionship. She loved the adoration of men. That may be one reason why she tried so desperately to please John and capture his love and interest. Although she probably never thought of John as more than a brother, she certainly did see in him a very wise, handsome, witty man on whom she could pour her affection without being misunderstood and without giving any long-term commitment. He, in turn, satisfied her need for male companionship.

In addition to the new curate, however, there were other love interests. One was a Mr. Johnson. Where or how she met him is not clear. Very little is known of Mr. Johnson, other than that he was passionately in love with Martha and that she at first responded coldly to his advances. Her response was conditioned partly because his family did not approve of her; but more importantly because he was not only poor, but had little prospect for any financial improvement in the future. Martha had seen enough of poverty, and was not about to yield too easily at this point.

This placed her in somewhat of a quandry. She apparently enjoyed being the center of his affection, but, knowing that she has no intention of ever marrying a man in Johnson's circumstances, she felt that she should not give him any encouragement. She therefore wrote him several discouraging letters. However, he refused to be discouraged and continued his advances until Martha clearly dismissed him.

Three months after this break Johnson wrote to her again, this time with a new note of optimism. His brother, who was in Orders, had married a lady with a private fortune of two thousand pounds and had promised to set him up in business.

Martha suddenly discovered she liked Johnson more than she had at first thought, and she wrote post haste to John for advice. The situation had evidently become critical because Johnson had announced his intention of visiting Martha at Epworth. She did not want to make a fool of Johnson by encouraging him if she had no intention of marrying him, but, if her father died, she would have no security whatsoever; Johnson then might well be a satisfactory port, if nothing else. "I may as well be contented with one I am not very fond of now as stay till I am destitute and maybe marry a man that neither loves me nor I him." (Green, p. 237)

We do not know how John responded other than that he suggested another possibility for Martha — a Matthew Horbery, a young Lincoln graduate with excellent prospects in the church. Martha had met Horbery and admitted there was wisdom in John's choice. However, he lacked one serious essential — he had no idea how to make love to a woman of Martha's passionate nature. She wrote to John:

> I really grant all you say of Mr. Horbery to be true! And if I can as you say, "converse with him without being worse," there is indeed no doubt but I may reap much profit, to say nothing of pleasure, by his conversation. (JWL, I, p. 272)

She went so far as to say that Horbery, when he visited her at the rectory, proved to be the best conversationalist she had ever known. On the other hand, she said that he was no more a lover than "a Grand Turk" (Green, p. 237).

After a time, both suitors relinquished the battle for Patty's hand, although Horbery remained on visiting terms with the Wesleys. Horbery's parents died early, leaving him an estate of four hundred pounds. He became Lincolnshire Fellow of Magdalene, and later married Sarah Taylor, a vicar's daughter. He became the Vicar of Eccleshall and Standlake and resigned his fellowship. His sermons were characterized by Samuel Johnson as "excellent" and the actor Garrick described him as "one of the best deliverers of a sermon he had ever heard." (Green, p. 133 N. and p. 237). Martha indeed had missed an opportunity for a rewarding and happy life when she turned her back on Horbery simply because he lacked, in her eyes, certain social graces.

During this period Martha had been spending some time visiting her Uncle Matthew in London so that she had a variety of interests besides her male companions and suitors, and life was a happier and pleasanter experience for her than previously. Nevertheless, she had moments of depression. John found her in one of these depressions at her Uncle Matthew's home in 1733. She still had not found a husband nor seemed to have any favorable prospects.

John talked to her very seriously, convincing her of the love of God and setting forth the virtues of the celibate life. Martha readily believed the former idea, but had no interest in the latter. She wanted a man, marriage, and security; not necessarily in that order, but certainly all three together. Celibacy had no charms for her, although John seemed to think he had convinced her of the virtues of the celibate state.

Shortly thereafter Martha was approached by yet another suitor, Benjamin Ingham, friend of John Wesley, a member of the Holy Club and later a missionary with John to the Indians in Georgia. John Wesley states in his diary, "Ingham in love with Sister Patty." (Heit, BI, p. 255 N.120). The affair did not last very long, and on Ingham's return from Georgia he eventually married Lady Margaret Hastings.

The Strange Courtship of Westley Hall

The man who eventually made the deepest impression on Martha was Westley Hall. Their courtship and married life is the strangest story of all the Wesley sisters.

Westley Hall was one of John Wesley's students at Lincoln College, Oxford. He was a handsome, well-mannered person who dressed impeccably and possessed a great deal of charm. Under Wesley's guidance he had enjoyed a religious experience that caused him to join the Holy Club called Methodists. Little is known of his background or family. They must have had some wealth or position, for later, after Hall had decided to accompany the Wesley brothers as a missionary to the Indians in Georgia, his family, having strongly objected, had had sufficient influence to secure an attractive cure for him at home.

Hall must have been a good student and a pious Methodist. He made a very favorable impression on John Wesley, himself, as well as on John's mother, Susanna. He was ordained as early as 1734, but he refused to accept a parish at that time. Susanna, in consternation, wrote to John:

> I cannot think Mr. Hall does well in refusing an opportunity of doing so much service to religion, as he certainly might do, if he accepted the living he is about to refuse. (Ty, *OM,* p. 387)

John, however, continued to look favorably on him and spoke of him as "holy and unblamable in all manner of conversation." (Ty, *OM,* p. 387)

Patty seems to have met Hall at the home of her Uncle Matthew while she was staying in London. He soon became her suitor. Patty, as we have seen, had had a succession of unsuccessful love affairs. By now, moreover, she was in her prime — beautiful, attractive, an excellent conversationalist with a matured outlook on life. She lacked only that sharp wit that characterized some of the Wesleys and was a prominent feature of eighteenth-century social life. She made up for this by her conversation and her exceedingly charming manner. She had also outgrown her tendency to complain constantly about her lot in life. She had written to John:

> You have so often blamed me for complaining that you have long since broke me of it. (JWL, I, P. 272)

This was not entirely accurate, but certainly Martha had matured in her attitude toward life and was doing a lot less complaining and showing a greater interest in others. She was surrounded by the love, security and social position provided by her Uncle Matthew and she radiated new confidence and poise. More than ever her appearance and manner explained why she had numerous suitors.

She was deeply impressed by the affable but serious-minded Westley Hall with his elegant manners and attractive appearance, and when Hall began to make love to Patty with a view to marriage, Patty was only too ready to respond.

When Hall pressed her to marry him, Patty accepted his proposal without consulting either her brother John or any other member of the Wesley household. This is not surprising when one remembers that her father had broken up her relationship with John Romley and that her brother, John, had not encouraged any intimacy with Johnson but had pressed upon her instead the claims of his friend, Matthew Horbery, whom Patty apparently thought of as stodgy. John had then suggested a life of celibacy, which was far from the mind and intention of the beautiful Martha Wesley.

Sometime after his proposal to Patty, Westley Hall accompanied John Wesley on a visit to Epworth. Here he met Kezia or "Kezzy", Patty's youngest sister. Very soon he was openly making advances to Kezzy. John Wesley noted Hall's conduct in his Journal:

> He took all the freedom with her that was consistant with modesty, and such as I thought her reserved temper would never have allowed to any but an actual husband. My father and mother soon observed it. He spoke to me, and my mother to him upon it. He told her what he had told my sister; from whom he could not now bear an hour's separation, insomuch that all the servants, as well as the occasional visitants that we had, began to ask 'When Miss Kezzy was to be married?' When we visited in any town, he was equally unreserved; and, my sister telling him that he showed his design to all the world, he answered, 'So much the better; I have no design but I would have all the world to know.'
>
> The day before we were to return to Oxford, I begged him once more seriously to consider what spirit it was he was moved by. He appeared very thoughtful all that day; but in the evening renewed his assurances to my sister that he would be hers, only hers, for ever. (JWJ, VIII, p. 147)*

John Wesley was astounded, partly because Westley Hall had previously openly boasted that he had received that particular gift mentioned by Jesus that would enable him to remain celibate. Mr. Clayton, another leader of the Holy Club, was likewise surprised and asked Hall whether or not he had made any promise of marriage. On receiving a negative answer Clayton pressed Hall to pray earnestly to learn whether celibacy was not the more excellent way.

Apparently John Wesley, in spite of Hall's statements, was uncertain whether or not any actual promises of marriage had been given and received by Kezzy and Westley Hall.

John Whitelamb, who had married Mary Wesley, had also watched the proceedings at Epworth between Kezzy and Hall, and he was persuaded that the two certainly planned marriage. He was, as we have seen, very angry at Kezzy for attempting to prevent his marriage to Mary. He now wrote several letters to Westley Hall attacking the character of Kezzy and urging Hall not to consider marrying her. Hall turned to John Wesley in this crisis. John strongly defended Kezzy. In the face of Whitelamb's accusations, however, Hall began to waver in his affection for Kezzy, and since he was now in easy reach of Patty Wesley in London, he began to renew his advances to her. She was apparently totally unaware of what had gone on at Epworth.

The whole affair is most confusing, and it is difficult to unravel the order of events or the motivations of the chief actors, especially since sections of John Wesley's Journal account of the affair are missing. Years later, John Wesley attempted to summarize the events in a letter to Westley Hall. (JWL, II, p. 269) In the following account I have attempted to combine Wesley's two versions, omitting tedious details and seeming contradictions.

Apparently at Epworth, Hall had vehemently told Wesley that God had made it plain to him that he was to marry Kezzy. After returning to London, however, Hall claimed to have received a counter-revelation that he was not to marry Kezzy but her sister Patty. This was in the face of a previous declaration that God had empowered him to become a eunuch for the sake of the Kingdom of Heaven. Apparently, either God or Westley Hall was having great difficulty in making up his mind.

Shortly before the death of their father, John and Charles Wesley returned to Epworth, accompanied by Westley Hall. Samuel, Sr. was happy to see his sons and especially grateful that Hall was with them. Both Patty and Kezzy were also at the Rectory. It would seem as though each believed she was engaged to Hall.

---

* From p. 147 to p. 152 Wesley writes in great detail concerning Hall and his affairs with both Kezzy and Martha. It is entitled "A Fragment," and unfortunately four pages of the fragment are missing. Many of the details are tedious and unnecessary to an understanding of the situation. (JWJ, VIII, p. 147)

Patty returned to London, and Westley Hall, remaining at Epworth, conversed very seriously with Kezzy. By this time she seemed to have been aware that Hall had made some kind of an advance to Patty, but she did not seem sure how far Hall's affair with Patty had progressed.

Later, on his return to London, John Wesley found Hall and Patty together. After Patty took her leave, John asked Hall what he intended doing. "Marry her!" Hall had answered. Then he showed John Wesley letters from John Whitelamb assassinating the character of Kezzy and suggesting that Hall marry Patty. John Wesley urged Hall not to act hastily. Hall then stated that he intended securing a license and asked John Wesley to marry him and Patty at once. John refused unless Hall had his mother's consent and the consent of Patty's Uncle Matthew. Hall proceeded to Tunbridge, where Matthew Wesley was then staying, to secure his consent. It is uncertain what happened at Tunbridge, but Hall eventually returned to make contact with John Wesley. He missed John at various places but met him at Salisbury. Here he again showed John letters from Whitelamb attacking Kezzy's character and supporting his accusations with purported proofs, all of which John Wesley flatly denied. Hall appeared shocked and stated that he must see Kezzy at once.

Hall left for a conference with Kezzy, who later told John that Hall had solemnly re-affirmed his love for her. He had also said that he was indeed sorry for any misunderstanding that had arisen over Patty, and he gave Kezzy a kind of friendship ring until he would be able to return and present her with a wedding ring.

This was in September of 1735. On the thirteenth of the same month Hall married Patty in London, much to the consternation of the entire Wesley family.

Apparently the family believed that Patty had somehow managed to steal Kezzy's fiance from her by playing on his affections while he was in London. Charles wrote Patty a stinging note including a long poem in which he charged her with incest (Clarke, p. 518f). Samuel, Jr., who had never liked Hall from his first meeting with him, looking upon him as a smooth-tongued hypocrite, was equally unhappy with the way things turned out. John also supported Kezzy against Patty, fully believing that Hall had acted in totally unworthy manner — which he had.

Patty eventually rose to her own defence. She bluntly stated that hers was the prior claim and that Hall had engaged himself to her even before he had ever met Kezzy. She also indicated that she had informed her mother of her plans and had secured the permission of her Uncle Matthew. Her mother had stated that if her uncle consented to the marriage, Patty should go ahead with her plans, which she did. Her Uncle gave her a wedding present of five hundred pounds. In short, Patty was charging that Kezzy had interfered with her love affair with Hall, especially since she had been engaged to Hall before Kezzy had met him.

John never fully accepted Patty's version of the whole matter, and some years later wrote Hall a letter in which he charged him with the death of Kezzy. He wrote among other things:

> The other [that is Kezzy] who had honored you as an angel from heaven, and still loved you much too well (for you had stole her heart from the God of her youth), refused to be comforted. From that time she fell into a lingering illness, which terminated in her death. And does not her blood still cry unto God from the earth? Surely it is upon your head. (JWLT, II, p. 112)

Wesley seems to have greatly overstated the case. Furthermore, he was writing to Hall a number of years after the events, when he and Hall had drifted far apart, both theologically and morally.

The fact is that the Wesleys, John and Kezzy included, had continued to be friends of Hall after his marriage to Patty, and the first shock of Hall's duplicity had worn off. Charles and John had accepted Hall as a possible missionary to the Indians when they decided to go to Georgia in the New World. Hall was determined to go with them in spite of the objections of his family and his bride. At the last minute, however, his uncle, his mother, and particularly Patty persuaded him to remain home. His uncle and his mother had been sufficiently influential to have secured an attractive cure or parish for him in Wootton-Rivers, a small village of about four hundred inhabitants in Wiltshire. Hall, much against his will, had consented to give up his plans for Georgia.

In his new parish, strange as it may seem, Hall not only took up residence with his wife Patty, but also with her sister Kezzy, who came to live with the happy couple. Far from being broken-hearted and falling into a lingering illness, as Wesley later indicated, Kezzy does not seem to have been too unhappy with the way things had turned out.

This may have been partly due to the fact that as early as June 16th, 1734 she had written to her brother John indicating that she was seriously considering the celibate way of life as the wiser choice. As time went on, the affair with Hall had apparently become a matter of indifference to her (See Chapter Eight for a further discussion of the situation). All the brothers, however, were furious with both Hall and Kezzy; with Hall for permitting Kezzy to live with him, and with Kezzy for agreeing to the strange arrangement. Samuel, Jr., her brother, cut Kezzy off completely for a time. He wrote to Charles, then in Georgia, "I have no correspondence with Kez: I did design it after reading yours; but the hearing that, she is gone to live with Patty and husband made me drop the design." (Ty, *OM*, p. 391)

In Kezzy's defense it should be noted that her father had died, her mother had gone elsewhere to live, and Kezzy had nowhere to go except to the home of her brother Samuel, who was ready to take her on condition that John would allow her fifty pounds a year toward her expenses. It would seem as though this allowance was not forthcoming from John, and facing a bleak future she chose, after a short stay with Samuel, to live with her sister and her former lover. The three got along very well.

By August, 1737, furthermore, Mrs. Wesley, herself, was also living with the Halls. Patty was her favorite daughter and she had always approved of Westley Hall, and now she wrote:

> Mr. Hall and his wife are very good to me. He behaves like a gentleman and a Christian; and my daughter with as much duty and tenderness as can be expressed. (Ty, *OM,* p. 392)

When John Wesley returned from Georgia he made arrangements for Kezzy to live with the Rev. Henry Piers, the Vicar of Bexley.

Westley Hall continued his work at Wootton-Rivers but by December 1737 he had moved to a church near Salisbury. Charles Wesley visited him here December 29th. Two years later Hall came to London. It is not known what church he served, but Mrs. Wesley continued to live with him and her daughter Patty.

Hall's ministry must have been fairly successful. John Wesley recorded an unusual incident that occurred in Hall's church and under Hall's ministry. He wrote:

> I talked largely with my mother, who told me, that, till a short time since, she had scarce heard such a thing mentioned as having God's Spirit bearing witness with our spirit: much less did she imagine, that, this was the common privilege of all true believers. 'Therefore,' she said, 'I never durst ask it for myself. But two or three weeks ago, while my son Hall was pronouncing those words, in delivering the cup to me, — The blood of our Lord Jesus Christ, which was given for thee, — the words struck my heart, and I knew, God, for Christ's sake, had forgiven me all my sins.' (JWJ, II, p. 267)

John and Charles Wesley at this time were engaged in theological disputes with the Moravians, and, at first, Westley Hall supported them against the Moravians and their strange doctrine of "stillness." In this doctrine the eighteenth century English Moravians stated that only through silence and quiet waiting for God could a soul obtain salvation. All good works, the means of grace, any seeking after faith were discouraged, and the seeker was urged simply to be still and wait for the salvation of God. The Wesleys abhorred the doctrine and eventually separated from the Moravians, Hall going with the Wesleys. In time, however, Hall returned to the Moravian fold and sharply criticized the Wesleys.

During these years the Halls were bereaved of a number of children who did not survive their infancy. Patty had proved as prolific as her mother had been, and the babies came to the Halls annually.

Mrs. Wesley died in 1742, after having left the Halls and taken up residence at the Foundery where her son John had built a chapel and work room, a preachers' house and an apartment for his mother, his sister Emily, and her favorite servant. Emily later moved to West Street, London. John, now having more room at the Foundery, invited the Halls to live at the Foundery. All of Patty's children were dead, and John probably thought she and her husband could be of help with the work at the Foundery. He wrote to Patty on November 17th, 1742. It was a letter outstanding in its tactlessness and insensitivity:

> Dear Sister, — I believe the death of your children is a great instance of the goodness of God toward you. You have often mentioned to me how much of your time they took up. Now that time is restored to you, and you have nothing to do but to serve the Lord without carefulness and without distraction, till you are sanctified in body, soul, and spirit.

> As soon as I saw Mr. Hall I invited him to stay at the Foundery; but he desired that I would have him excused. There is a strange inconsistency in his tempers and sentiments with regard to me. (JWL, II, p. 91)

Wesley went on to describe his and Hall's relationship with the Moravians. He believed naively enough that Hall had been deceived by the Moravian teaching and that sooner or later he would return to the Wesleys.

> There remains in him something of his old regard for me, which he had at Oxford; and by and by it will prevail. He will find out these wretched men, and the clouds will flee away. (JWL, II, p. 91)

The letter was written in a kindly spirit and was meant both to comfort Patty on the successive loss of her children and to explain why John had not been successful in securing Hall's services at the Foundery. His explanation with regard to the Foundery is clearly stated, but no one can congratulate him on the manner in which he tried to comfort Patty on her continuing griefs. It is doubtful if, from the beginning of time, any pastor except John Wesley, would have tried to comfort a mother by assuring her that the loss of her children is a "great instance of the goodness of God."

Patty, however, understood her brother, and she does not seem to have objected to his apparently callous approach. She was not even hurt by his total lack of sensitivity. She realised that underlying his tactlessness was a deep concern for her welfare. She probably was more upset by her husband's refusal to accept John's gracious offer to live at the Foundery and assist in the work.

Patty and The Dissenters

Shortly before or about this time — 1742 — Westley Hall apparently left his parish in London and went to Salisbury. Here he set up a Society of his own, persuading everyone connected with his chapel to forsake the Anglican Church and become Dissenters. Patty, however, remained loyal to the Church. She was a Wesley and an Anglican, and despite great pressure from her husband and his converts, she remained an Anglican. Charles Wesley visited the Halls and noted in his *Journal*:

> 1743, August 11. From ten to two I got with my sister Hall in Salisbury. She stands alone. Every soul of her husband's Society has forsaken the ordinances of God; for which reason she refuses to belong to it. (Ty, *OM*, p. 397)

Nearly two years later Charles Wesley was again in Salisbury and noted:

> I found my sister as a rock in the midst of waves. Mr. Hall's Society had all left the Church, and mocked and persecuted her for not leaving it. . . . At four I set out with my sister and reached Bristol in the afternoon of the next day. (Ty, *OM*, p. 397)

Six months later Hall tried unsuccessfully to persuade the Wesleys to leave the Church of England or at least to give up or abandon out-door preaching, the use of lay-evangelists, the administration of the sacraments in unconsecrated chapels, and the doctrine of Apostolic Succession. Wesley sent him a lengthy reply carefully outlining his ideas on these and other subjects.

On July 20th, 1746 Wesley noted in his *Journal.*

> I set out for Salisbury, where, to my utter amazement, Mr. Hall desired me to preach. Was his motive only, to grace his own cause? Or rather, was this the last gasp of expiring love? (Ty, *OM*, p. 400)

It is difficult to say what motivated Hall. Probably he still had an affection for his former teacher; but by now his true character was beginning to show in a startling manner. A little more than a year after his invitation to Wesley to preach in his Chapel, he abandoned his wife and family. According to the *Gentleman's Magazine,* he had drawn "multitudes of the meaner sort, both of Dissenters and the Established Church, to attend him." He had so bewitched his followers that they placed greater weight on his sermons than on the words of Christ and the Apostles. He compounded his heresies by first taking formal leave of his congregation and then deserting his wife and family. Before leaving his house he stripped his wife of all her childbed linen, and whatever he could conveniently turn into money, leaving her in deep distress. The Magazine adds these pregnant words:

> The fire of jealousy has broken out in many families, where *wives* or *daughters* were his followers. (Ty, *OM*, p. 400)

The innuendo of the statement is clear enough, and in the light of subsequent events, probably true. Later, however, Hall returned once again to the parish, and in 1748 turned his own wife out of his house temporarily, along with her brother John, who had come to Salisbury for a talk with him. (JWJ, Jan. 25, 1748)

Obviously womanizing was only one among Hall's numerous peccadillos. It is difficult to say whether or not Patty was aware of his weakness for women before it became generally known. Like her sister, Susanna, she never maligned her husband or publicly criticized him. One of his more flagrant affairs occurred at Salisbury. He became involved with a petite, attractive seamstress employed by his wife in their home. When the girl became pregnant and the time for her delivery drew near, Hall conveniently found some business that had to be cared for in London. When the seamstress fell into labor, Patty ordered one of the servants to fetch a mid-wife. The servant refused. In fact, none of the servants would have anything to do with the girl. Patty was shocked! She could not understand their attitude until one of them told her mistress that the father of the child was Patty's husband. The servants had known of the affair for some time, and they were disgusted with both Hall and his paramour.

In this crisis Patty, herself, went for a mid-wife, saw to it that the little seamstress was properly cared for, and then went up to London to contact her husband and bring him home. There is reason to believe that Patty's brothers took care of the seamstress and her child for some time.

Hall was deeply impressed by his wife's tolerance and generosity, and gave up his philandering, but not for long. He soon returned to his former ways. He again became intimate with his wife's seamstress, and when Hall finally abandoned her, John Wesley assisted her and her child financially as far as he was able. Patty also continued to help her.

On one occasion Hall brought home one of his bastard infants and ordered his wife to care for it, which she did. She brought a cradle and, placing the baby in it, provided in every way for its comfort. On another occasion she financially assisted another of her husband's concubines. Her brother Charles was completely mystified, and asked her how she could do such a thing. She answered, "I knew I could obtain what I wanted from many; but she, poor hapless creature, could not, many thinking it meritorious to abandon her to the distress she brought upon herself. *Pity* is due to the wicked; the good claim *esteem*. Besides I did not act as a *woman* but as a Christian." (Stev, p. 372)

Patty's generosity was characteristic of her personality. Charles once said that it was in vain to give Patty anything to add to her comforts, for she always gave it away to some person poorer than herself.

These instances were but a few of Hall's many acts of philandering. John Wesley in 1747 had taken the time and trouble to list a few of Hall's numerous adventures. He sought, thereby, to trace Hall's gradual fall, beginning with the fact that not only did his seriousness decline, but he began very frequently to kiss the women of the Society, and sometimes to take them in his arms, telling them that this was Christian fellowship, and a part of the communion of the saints. He evidently beguiled an Elizabeth Greenaway, a woman of great piety, who was at first shocked at Hall's advances, but who was won over by this "spiritual approach" until Hall was able to do everything he wished with her short of making her pregnant. One of his servants whom he sought to seduce broke loose from him and ran away. But he convinced a Ruth Whitehart who came to consult with him about a bodily illness that she had a stone, and that having a child would cure her. He then lay with her and let her go. There is no record as to whether the cure was successful or whether the woman ever had her child.

It was not long before Hall became a polygamist, openly preaching the doctrine of multiple wives. Adam Clarke, one of the first biographers of the Wesley family, wrote:

> Mr. Hall who was a clergyman in the church of England, . . . became a *Moravian,* and *Quietist,* an *Antinomian, a Diest* (if not an *Atheist*) and a *Polygamist,* which last he defended in his teaching and illustrated by his *practice.* (Clarke, p. 526)

Hall would leave his wife for months at a time, and, on returning was often abusive and quarrelsome. If she were not at home he would search for her.

In 1750 Patty appeared, quite unexpectedly, in the preaching house at Bristol. Charles Wesley provided a room for her. But the impetuous Hall had followed her, and Charles noted in his *Journal.*

> I had begun preaching, when Mr. Hall walked up the room, and through the desk, and carried her off with him (CWJ, II, p. 75).

On two occasions, possibly more, Patty sought to leave him permanently. Each time she wrote him. The first time she stated:

> Being at last convinced that I cannot possibly oblige you any longer by anything I can say or do, I have for some time determined to rid you of so useless a burden, as it should please God to give me an opportunity. If you have so much humanity left for a wife who has lived so many years with you as to allow anything toward a maintenance, I will thank you. (Ty, *OM,* p. 410)

The maintenance, however, does not seem to have been provided, and Patty returned to her husband. Sometime later, however, she made a final break, although she left the door open for a possible reconciliation. She wrote to Hall:

> Though I should have been very glad to have heard from you, yet I cannot wonder at your not answering my letter seeing I not only left you a second time, but desired conditions which I fear you do not find yourself at all disposed to grant. Indeed, I am obliged to plead guilty to the charge; and as I look upon you as the sole judge, I shall make no appeal from that sentence, only I desire to speak a few words before you pass it. You may remember, whenever I was angry enough to talk of leaving you, you could never work me up to such a height as to make me say I would never return. (Stev, p. 372f.)

Patty does not say what the conditions were that she had laid down for her return and for their reconciliation, but she was right in believing that Hall would never agree to them. He apparently did not respond to her letter, and soon afterward he went to Ireland from where he left for the West Indies, accompanied by one of his numerous "wives." He completely abandoned Patty, his first wife, although in a short note to her, he states he has provided for her welfare. There is no extant evidence of this so-called provision. He probably tried his best to forget her.

When his concubine died in the West Indies, Westley Hall returned to London. Henry Moore one of the early biographers of John Wesley states that on his return to England, Hall and Patty were again reunited, and that she took care of him until he died on January 3, 1776.

Moore's account is not documented in any way, and, at least one biographer, Maldwyn Edwards, thought it more likely that Hall and Patty never saw each other again after his journey to the West Indies. (ED, *FC*, p. 149)

Another folk tale states that on his death-bed Hall said, in speaking of Patty, "I have injured an angel! An angel that never reproached me!" Later biographers pounced upon these words and elaborated on them. One of them stated that these words made up to Mrs. Hall for all the sorrow he had caused her. (ED, *FC*, p. 149)

It is doubtful if Hall ever made the supposed statement, and it is doubtful whether he ever saw Patty on his return to England. The story makes excellent copy, however, and was included by Eliza Clarke in her *Life of Susanna Wesley*. However, Patty was far too sensible a woman to have been much comforted by the dying statement of a compulsive liar, adulterer, and wife beater.

She had lived with her husband on and off for forty years. She had ten children, most of whom died in their infancy. One child, a boy, lived till about fourteen years of age. He was taken from the Halls by John and Charles Wesley, who paid for his education. Unfortunately, he died of smallpox, adding another burden of grief to his mother's life. Charles Wesley remembered him in *Funeral Hymns*. Two of the hymns refer directly to the little lad, at least in their opening lines:

> Where is the fair Elysian flower,
> The blooming youth that charmed our eyes?
> Cut down and withered in an hour,
>   But now transplanted to the skies.
> His triumph o're the moldering tomb —
> He blossoms in eternal bloom!

The second hymn begins:

> Rest, happy saint! with God Secure,
>   Lodged in the bosom of the Lamb;

> Thy joy is full, thy state is sure,
>   Through all eternity the same;
> The heavenly doors have shut thee in,
> The mighty gulf is fixed between.

The last lines of this stanza suggest that a gulf was fixed between the boy and his father who had evidently not treated him very well, although they might as readily refer to the gulf between life and death.

John Wesley, nevertheless, believed that Hall had deeply repented before he died. He wrote in his *Journal*:

> Tuesday, January 2, 1776 — I came [to Bristol] just time enough, not to see, but to bury poor Mr. Hall, my brother-in-law, who died on Wednesday morning; I trust in peace, for God had given him deep repentance. Such another monument of divine mercy, considering how low he had fallen, and from what heights of holiness, I have not seen, no, not in seventy years! I had designed to have visited him in the morning; but he did not stay for my coming. It is enough if, after all his wanderings, we meet again in Abraham's bosom. (JWJ, VI, p. 91)

He does not mention anything about Hall's last words which would certainly have been reported to him, and which he would probably have related as a proof of Hall's deep repentance. He is also silent concerning the possible presence of his sister, Patty.

Happier Days

Patty's search for love had ended in the futility of death—Hall's death, but this did not break her spirit. She moved forward in a search possibly for a deeper love than Hall could ever have extended to her.

Her financial needs were taken care of by her brothers, John and Charles Wesley, who also saw to it that she always had a comfortable place to live. She lived for a time with her sister Emily at her rooms in West Street, London. She also began to develop her friendship with Dr. Samuel Johnson, the English lexicographer. Where and when she met him is not known, except that Sarah Wesley, the daughter of Charles, stated that:

> Dr. Johnson was an early friend of hers; to her my father owed his acquaintance with the Doctor, and I, the honor of his favor. I used to accompany her to Bolt Court, and had the privilege of hearing their discourse. (Ty, *OM,* p. 410)

Sarah's brother Charles Wesley, Jr. supports this story in a letter to Dr. Adam Clark in which he relates some incidents in the life of Sarah when she was but a child.

> Dr. Johnson much distinguished my sister in her youth. She was not, like many others, afraid of him; indeed the doctor was always gentle to children; and no doubt my aunt Hall [Patty Wesley Hall] had spoken kindly to him of her. She used to show him her verses, and he would pat her head and say to my aunt, "Madam, she will do." (Stev, p. 475)

Dr. Adam Clarke in his volume on *Memoirs of the Wesley Family* refers to Patty Hall's friendship with Samuel Johnson. He provides no documentation for his statements but he may have heard the stories from Patty's niece in whom she confided or they may have been common knowledge among the Wesleys. At any rate, Clarke wrote:

> She spent much time, at his own particular request, with Dr. *Samuel Johnson*, who was strongly attached to her, and ever treated her with high reverence and respect.
>
> . . .
> They often disputed together on matters of *Theology* and *Moral Philosophy*; and in their differences of opinion, for they often differed, he never treated *her* with that asperity with which he often treated . . . opponents. He wished her very much to become an inmate in his house; and she would have done so, had she not feared to provoke the jealousy of the two females already there, Mrs. Williams and Mrs. Du Moulin, who had long resided under his roof.
>
> . . .
> In his house at Bolt-Court, one day when Mrs. Hall was present, the Doctor began to expatiate on the unhappiness of human life. Mrs. Hall said, 'Doctor, you have always lived among the *wits*, not the *saints*; and they are a race of people the most unlikely to seek true happiness, or find the pearl without price.'
>
> . . .
> In a conversation there was a remark made, that the *public voice* was the voice of *truth*, universally recognized; whence the proverb, *Vox populi, vox Dei*. This Mrs. Hall strenuously contested; and said the "*public voice*" in Pilate's Hall was *Crucify Him! Crucify Him!* (Clarke, p. 532f)

Patty also appeared in Boswell's *Johnson*, but always under the name of Mrs. Hall.

Boswell records some conversation that took place in 1781:

> Our company consisted of Mrs. Williams, Mrs. Desmoulins, Mr. Levett, Mr. Allen, the printer, (Mr. Macbean), and Mrs. Hall, sister of the Reverend Mr. John Wesley, and resembling him, as I thought, both in figure and manner. Johnson produced now, for the first time, some handsome silver salvers, which he told me he had bought fourteen years ago; so it was a great day. . . .
>
> I mentioned a kind of religious Robinhood Society, which met every Sunday evening at Coachmakers' hall, for free debate; and that the subject for this night was, the text which relates, with other miracles that happened at our Saviour's death, "And the graves were opened, and many bodies of the saints which slept arose, and came out of the graves after His resurrection, and went into the holy city, and appeared unto many." Mrs. Hall said it was a very curious subject, and she would like to hear it discussed. Johnson (somewhat warmly) "One would not go to such a place to hear it, — one would not be seen in such a place — to give countenance to such a meeting." I, however, resolved that I would

go. "But Sir, (said she to Johnson,) I should like to hear you discuss it." He seemed reluctant to engage in it. She talked of the resurrection of the human race in general, and maintained that we shall be raised with the same bodies. Johnson, "Nay, Madam, we see that it is not to be the same body; for the Scripture uses the illustration of grain sown, and we know that the grain which grows is not the same with what is sown. You cannot suppose that we shall raise with a diseased body; it is enough that there be such a sameness as to distinguish identity of person." She seemed desirous of knowing more, but he left the question in obscurity. . . .

Some time after this, upon his making a remark which escaped my attention, Mrs. Williams and Mrs. Hall were both together trying to answer him. He grew angry, and called out loudly, "Nay, when you both speak at once, it is intolerable." But checking himself and softening, he said, "This one may say, though you *are* ladies. Then he brightened into gay humour, and addressed them in the words of one of the songs in "The Beggar's Opera."

"But two at a time there's no mortal can bear."

"What, Sir, (said I,) are you going to turn Captain Macheath?" There was something as pleasantly ludicrous in this scene as can be imagined. the contrast between Macheath, Polly, and Lucy—and Dr. Samuel Johnson, blind, peevish Mrs. Williams, and lean, lank, preaching Mrs. Hall, was exquisite. (Bos, III, pp. 160, 161)

In Chapter Ten of Cassell's *Old and New London*, the group as described by Boswell, appears as a full-page illustration. Johnson seems to be rolling in his chair; Boswell is holding his chin as if listening; Mr. Levett looks sour and perplexed; and Frank, the black servant, proudly attends the company with the silver salvers. The women complete the scene.

Patty had a keen mind and a retentive memory. She recalled long passages of books and plays that she had read, and her converstaion was never boring. She was, however, a daughter of the eighteenth century, and she believed that the scripture revealed that God had given the husband authority over his wife. She was surprised that anyone would dispute this idea. "It is so clearly expressed in the Scripture, that one would suppose such wives had never read their Bibles." (Stev, p. 379)

Like her brother John, she loved order, insisting that "Order is Heaven's first Law." She despised the works of Jonathan Swift, and thought that his *Tale of a Tub* was irreverent and not to be atoned for by its wit. She was herself a very devout person, and although she was a staunch Anglican, she professed having had a Methodist type personal experience of religion. On Good Friday, April 12th, 1744, she wrote in her *Journal*:

Near a year ago, I was one evening retired into my chamber, with a design to spend some time in private prayer; but before I kneeled down, all at once (without a thought of mine) I had a full clear sense that the Lamb of God had made an atonement for me; that he had made full satisfaction for my sins; so that, were He that moment to appear in judgment, I could stand before Him. (Stev, p. 382)

When commenting one day to a friend about her many trials and troubles she said, "Evil was not kept from me; but evil has been kept from harming me." (Stev, p. 380)

As she grew older she grew calm, strong and, in some ways, quite stubborn. She often took long walks throughout the city, much to the consternation of her family and friends. She never hurried at the crossings even though carriages were all about her. Her niece Sarah once tried to hurry her out of the way when they were walking together in Bloomsbury Square and a coach was closely following them. Her niece pulled her along so strongly she caused her to fall. When Patty arose and had brushed off her dress, she said quite calmly, "the probability of being injured by a fall is greater than being run over by coachmen who could gain no advantage by it; on the contrary much disadvantage and expense." (Stev, p. 380)

The ageing Patty was very close to Sarah, her niece, and told her many things about her own long life. Her niece wanted especially to be with her aunt when she died. Patty smiled and said, "Yes, you may be with me if you are able to bear it; but I charge you not to grieve for me more than half an hour."

Shortly before she died on July 12th, 1791, she called to Sarah and said, "I have now a sensation that convinces me my departure is near; the heartstrings seem gently but entirely loosened."

When asked if she were in pain, she replied, "No but a new feeling." Her niece stated that her aunt had no disease, but a mere decay of nature.

Just before she closed her eyes she bade her niece come near: she pressed her hand, and said, "I have the assurance which I have long prayed for. Shout!" and she expired. (Stev, p. 381)

Her search for love was ended, or perhaps just beginning.

She was buried in the same vault with her brother John in the burial ground of Wesley's Chapel, City Road, London.

In *The Gentleman's Magazine* her obituary notice read:

1791. July 12, in the City Road, in her eighty-fourth year, Mrs. Martha Hall, widow of the Rev. Mr. H., and last surviving sister of Rev. John and Charles Wesley. She was equally distinguished by piety, understanding, and sweetness of temper. Her sympathy for the wretched, and her bounty, even to the worthless, will eternise her memory in better worlds than this. (Ty, *OM,* p. 411)

From an old print.
An attractive street scene in old London.

Chapter Eight

Quiet Desperation
The Story of Kezia Wesley

Kezia Wesley led a life of quiet desperation. She was the last child born to her mother when Susanna was about forty years old. There is no extant record of her birth or baptism. It is generally thought she was born sometime in 1709 or 1710. Originally it had been thought she was born shortly after the parsonage fire in 1709. Indirect evidence of this date was found in a letter from Samuel Wesley, Sr. to the Duke of Buckingham. He wrote that Mrs. Wesley was then near her confinement, and he hoped that she would not miscarry due to the fright and peril of the rectory fire, but that she would bring him his nineteenth child. The child was probably not Kezia, but an unnamed baby who was in reality the eighteenth child.

It is an amazing fact, attested by some of today's Wesleyan scholars, that the Wesleys were never quite sure how many children they actually produced—eighteen or nineteen. Perhaps this is not as surprising as it seems. Susanna's father, when he was asked how many children he had, would answer that he had either two dozen or twenty-five.

There are no extant records of the birthdates of Kezia or her brother Charles. Charles' record was destroyed in the rectory fire, but since Kezia was born after the fire, it is curious that her record does not appear in a later registry. Charles was never certain of his birth date and once wrote to his brother John seeking to clarify the matter. In reply, John stated, "My sister Kezia was born about March 1710; therefore you could not have been born later than December 1708." (JWLT, V, p. 330) Recent research sets the baptismal date for Charles as December 29th, 1707. There is no extant baptismal record for Kezia. A transcript of Charles' baptismal record was found in the archives of the Bishop of Lincoln.

Childhood and Early Life

Susanna began the formal education of each of her children when he or she was five years of age; but in the case of Kezia she states that she was over-ruled—by whom is not clear—and Kezia joined the group earlier. Susanna implies that Kezia's earlier start was not particularly helpful to her for "she was more years in learning than any of the rest had been months." (Stev, p. 415)

This may have been because when Kezia was placed in school Susanna was concentrating a great deal of attention upon John who was preparing to leave for Charterhouse in London. He entered Charterhouse in 1714. Later Susanna concentrated on Charles. Kezia was not openly neglected, but certainly she was not given the same patient teaching that had marked the training of her brothers and sisters. She probably was left to shift for herself. After all, her mother was past forty years of age and had given birth to nineteen children. She can be forgiven if she began to take a little less interest in teaching and training. However, Kezia's letters in her maturity reveal a style and love for learning that was the mark of all the Wesleys.

As a child she seems to have been carefree and independent. After "Old Jeffrey" began haunting the parsonage, Kezia, instead of becoming frightened tried rather to frighten her sister Patty by coming up behind her and stamping on the floor in imitation of the ghost. Imagine Kezia's surprise when the poltergeist responded in the same place with three knocks.

On another occasion Kezia was actually eager for some contact with "Old Jeffrey."

She said, "Let it answer me too if it can!"

She then stamped with her foot upon the floor and she and Jeffrey stamped back and forth several times.

She was present when Anne's bed was levitated, but she seems to have forgotten the incident; for when she was questioned years later she said, "I remember nothing else, but that it knocked my father's knock one night in the nursery, ready to beat the house down." (Stev, p. 416)

Her failure of memory is not surprising when one remembers she was only about six years of age during the hauntings. Little more is known about Kezia's childhood.

Maturity and the Endless Quest

Not much is known about the maturity of Kezia and the endless search in which she joined her sisters in their quest for love. Few of her letters are extant, and there are not many references to her in the letters and journals of her brothers.

In a letter to her brother John written when she was about nineteen years old she refers in mysterious terms to what may have been a love affair with an unnamed suitor.

The letter was written from Lincoln. Having received training similar to that of her sisters, she was prepared to serve as a teacher or governess herself. She joined the school of Mrs. Taylor where Emily was a teacher, and served as a pupil-teacher, both teaching and receiving instruction for her board and lodging but without any allowance for clothes. Like all the Wesley sisters, she wrote in a neat, clear hand. Her letters are formed in a square upright manner that is a style of writing distinctly her own and very readable.

Kezia does not explain in her letter what had actually happened between her and the possible youthful suitor. However, throughout the letter she seems somewhat bitter and certainly disillusioned. She writes also with a kind of tolerant irony. John had apparently recommended a young man for her consideration. She replied:

If I was inclined to enter into the holy state of matrimony, I can't say but the man you are acquainted with might be worthy of love.

> But to a soul whose marble form
> None of the melting passions warm,

all his good qualities would appear lighter than vanity itself. It is my humble opinion that I shall live the life of a nun, for which reason I would not give one single farthing to see him this minute. But if the young man were ever to have an inclination for any of our family, there is a certain lady at Epworth who would make a very good wife, and seems not averse to marriage, that would be worth his acceptance; besides, it would make her amends for a sort of baulk which I fancy she has had lately. There is but one objection against it, which is that it is twenty to one he will never see her. (Stev, pp. 416, 417)

The passage is difficult to interpret. Kezia might be referring to one of her sisters who had received a "sort of baulk," or, what is more likely, she might be referring to herself.

In any case, someone's love affair has evidently been broken up, and it might well have been Kezia's.

She then turns to a more religious situation personified in her fear of death.

> I am at present fearful of death; but I hope it will please God to make me willing and ready to die before he calls me out of the world.
> None know what death is but the dead;
> Therefore we all by nature dying dread
> As a strange doubtful path we know not how to tread.
> (Stev, p. 417)

It is difficult to imagine these passages being written by a teen-ager. Her pessimism is a little surprising but not inexplicable. She was greatly depressed by her surroundings — Mrs. Taylor, as we have seen in the sketch of the life of Emily, was not a pleasant person to work for; this in itself would depress even a more matured person. In addition Kezia faced poverty and a bleak future.

She continued her letter in the same vein, and she called John to task for something he had written, probably in the spirit of fun. It did not please Kezia.

> . . . there was one passage in it which I disliked. If you meant it as a banter, it was not kind, because nobody is worthy such a one for not having a beautiful face or a fine shape, it being only the gift of nature, · and not to be acquired. If you intended it for a compliment, it was still unkind. Perhaps you might think it would please the vanity of our sex to be flattered. Know, then, that I am not yet vain enough to be pleased with flattery. I hope your goodness will pardon my freedom. I should not have told you what I disliked, only by way of prevention, that you might not write after the same manner for the future. (Stev, p. 417)

She continued her letter by asking John to assist her in improving herself, especially in virtue by giving her good advice and telling her of her faults.

Again the pessimism shows through her letter when she speaks critically of her father for not having supplied her with clothes suitable for her position:

> It would be no great matter if my father was to find me in clothes for three or four years, since he pays nothing for my board. There is one comfort, which is that I can't be blamed if I go home, because it is not possible for me to stay without necessaries.
>
> Suppose my sister would find me in clothes, which I have no reason to expect, nor do I believe it is in her power if it was in her will, I could not be tolerably easy to be kept by any relation but my father or mother while they live. I believe it is chiefly owing to pride, and a little to the shyness of my natural temper. It was always pain to me to ask for my own, and it would be much worse if I knew I was a burden to any of my relations. I shall endeavor to be as easy as possible, —
>
> Nor think it chance, nor murmur at the load;
> For, know, what man calls fortune, is from God.
> (Stev, p. 417)

Throughout the letter she scatters some information about the family at Epworth and the villagers:

Dick Ellison had been quarrelling again with his wife, Susanna; although apparently this is so common she did not see the need for adding any details. She noted that "Mr. Barry is dead." "John Pindar is married to Mrs. Medley. Poor soul! I don't envy her choice."

She asks John to show her letter to Charles, probably to save her writing another lengthy note.

The letter is shattering in its revelation of the poverty of the Wesley family and its effect on Kezia, the youngest of all the Wesley sisters.

In July 1729 Kezia wrote another long letter to John. Apparently she had been neglectful of her correspondence and says that she is writing now only because he has "threatened to deprive me of the satisfaction of hearing from you anymore . . ."(Stev, p. 418)

Kezzy had not written to John for about six months, although he had apparently written to her on several occasions. For a person who professed to love her brother as Kezzy claimed, and for a person who was as lonely and ill-cared for as Kezzy had indicated in her previous letter, it is difficult to understand why she had not written sooner.

One reason may be because she was suffering from a decided inferiority complex, another because her situation had not changed for the better.

She referred to herself as an illiterate person. She wrote:

> I could not have imagined that it would be any pleasure to a person of sense to hear from such an illiterate person, had I not had it from your own hand and seal. (Stev, p. 418)

Later in the letter she wrote:

> . . . you know that our sex have naturally weaker minds than yours. (Stev, p. 418)

She was still deeply depressed. Her sister Sukey (Susanna) had been very ill and Kezzy hoped that Sukey would go "where the wicked cease from troubling, and the weary are at rest." (Stev, 418)

Her mother was also quite ill, probably because of "her want of clothing or convenient meat." Kezzy was also concerned for her own ill-health "constant these three years." All these burdens weighed upon her

> . . . For who can undergo the force
> Of present ills with fears of future woe?

Then Kezzy added a curious note:

> I beg you will tell my brother Charles I cannot always excuse him for writing, though I do it now. I am very sorry he meets with so many misfortunes, and wish it was in my power to alleviate them. (Stev, p. 418)

It would seem as though Kezzy had been writing to Charles who had not responded. She evidently liked Charles better than John, and as time went on they became very close friends.

Eighteen months later Kezzy again wrote to John—this time from Epworth, for she had returned home. She was concerned because she had not heard from John. She had evidently written to him without receiving a response.

> Had anybody told me you would have been almost four months without writing, and confirmed it with an oath, I should not have believed it; nor if I had not loved you with more than a sister's love, 'tis likely I should never have written more.

Once again her sense of inferiority is evident as she added, "Perhaps you may say you should not have cared if I never had." (Stev, p. 419)

She had come home because she had not sufficient money to buy those things necessary to her as a teacher-student at Lincoln. Her brother Samuel had sent her five pounds but Emily, her sister, had kept the money in part payment of what was owing to her on Kezzy's account.

Kezzy was not angry at this high-handed conduct of Emily and added, "nor do I blame her." Nevertheless, Samuel's well meant gesture was wasted, and Kezzy returned to Epworth.

Her letter included references to the situation at Epworth and in the village and also referred again to a mysterious love affair that she might have had that ended on a sour note.

> Dear brother, for your sake I intend to be careful of loving again, for whoever we take pleasure in are certainly capable of giving us pain;

After this reference to some past love affair she added a line that demonstrated once more her lack of self-esteem:

> nor should I ever have thought of choosing you as a friend when there was so great inequality between us, if you had not told me that "love, like death, makes all distinctions void." (Stev, p. 420)

The paragraph possibly explains why she eventually drew closer to her brother Charles. Charles was nearer her age, whereas John was considerably older than she and was well established in his career. Naturally she felt, what we would term, the generation gap, but which she called "inequality."

By 1731 she was back in Lincoln again, and she wrote to her brother John enlisting his aid in suggesting books for her to read. Her letter carries the pitiable statement that it was exceedingly difficult for her to secure books. At Epworth, of course, she had the use of her father's fairly well-stocked library, but here at Lincoln she had only two books, Nelson's *Method of Devotion* and *The Whole Duty of Man*—certainly not the most exciting reading, nor even the most challenging.

Then she indicated what to us would be an amusing and surprising confession—Kezzy was a user of snuff. She wrote:

> Pray desire brother Charles to bring "Prior," the second part, when he comes; or send it, according to promise, for leaving off snuff till next May, or else I shall think myself at liberty to take as soon as I please. (Stev, p. 421)

The rector, himself, was the only one of the Wesleys who used any form of tobacco, and he wrote a poem on the delights of a pipe of tobacco on a cold winter morning; but there is no extant record of any other of the Wesleys using tobacco in any form, and Kezzy's use of snuff must have been alarming to Charles to cause him to promise a copy of Prior's poems to Kezzy if she left off the habit for a time, at least.

Charles evidently looked upon the use of snuff as we might today look upon the use of marijuana.

Maybe she used snuff as a form of exhilaration to overcome her depressions, or because she was constantly ill. She closed her letter by writing, "I am ill, and can't write anymore."

Shortly after writing this letter, Kezzy returned once more to Epworth. Both her parents were ill and infirm; her sisters were married or teaching, and Martha was in London keeping house for her Uncle Matthew. Kezzy was really the only sister in a position to assist her parents, and as a loyal member of the family, she stepped in and helped.

The Coming of Westley Hall — the Heart-breaker

It is not difficult to imagine how lonely Kezzy must have been at Epworth, where she now carried the full responsibility for running the household. Each day was much like the last, except probably more burdensome. She, like Macbeth, could say,

Tomorrow and tomorrow and tomorrow, creeps
on this petty pace.

When, therefore, John came to Epworth for a visit, bringing with him a handsome, charming, serious-minded student, Kezzy was aroused out of her lethargy. Westley Hall, the student, could not have arrived at a more opportune time had he planned to win the heart and hand of Kezzy Wesley in marriage. Unfortunately, for any ideas that may have entered his mind about Kezzy, he was already contracted to or engaged to Martha Wesley, whom he had met at her uncle's house in London.

However, in spite of her inferiority complex and her apathetic approach to life, Kezzy must still have been a beautiful woman. At least, when Hall was in her presence he seemed to forget all about Martha in London. Kezzy, in return, responded to his advances quite readily, since they were made on a very high plane. Once, as we have seen, she had sharply rebuked her brother John for idle compliments which she believed were neither sincere nor flattering. Had Hall approached Kezzy with comments about her beauty or the qualities of her mental endowments, she probably would have repulsed him. He used neither of these ploys. He apparently always addressed her quite seriously and wove a religious note into all his wooing. He assured her he was seeking her love not so much because of her beauty, but because it was the will of God. He was ready to let the whole world know of his affection for her because he thought their union had been sealed in Heaven. At least, this is what he indicated to John and most likely to Kezzy herself. This approach would have made a strong appeal to Kezzy, and we can easily understand why she fell so deeply in love with him.

The story of Hall's courtship has already been related in the chapter on Martha Wesley and need not be repeated here. However, there are a few facts that should be added to that narrative.

The first is that Kezzy was still as uncertain as ever about her own desirability. She still had a serious inferiority complex. It was difficult for her to believe that a man as handsome, charming and brilliant as Westley Hall could ever be seriously interested in her, and she was very much afraid that she could never measure up to his expectations as a wife. As late as June 16th, 1734, she wrote of her fears to John:

> I am as indifferent as it is lawful for any person to be whether I ever change my state or not, because I think a single life is the more excellent way; and there are also several reasons why I rather desire to continue as I am. One is, because I desire to be entirely disengaged from the world; but the chief is, I am so well apprised of the great duty a wife owes to her husband, that I think it almost impossible she should ever discharge it as she ought. But I can scarce say that I have the liberty of choosing,

for my relations are continually soliciting me to marry. I shall endeavor
to be as resigned and cheerful as possible to whatever God is pleased
to ordain for me. (Stev, p. 423)

We know that Westley Hall, after he returned to London, took up his
affair once again with Martha, and, during the succeeding months, he
vacillated between the two sisters—Kezzy and Martha. A few weeks before
he married Martha in London, he had sworn to marry Kezzy, sealing his
promise with the gift of a ring which he promised would soon be replaced
by a wedding ring.

John Wesley believed for a time that Kezzy's early death at thirty-two
years of age was caused by Westley Hall's cruel dissimulation. But this is
to be doubted, since Kezzy later accepted an invitation to live with the Halls,
following the death of her father.

Another thing that should be remembered is that Kezzy was ill throughout
most of her life. She was tired, ill, and in the state where she did not seem
to care what became of her. It is possible, therefore, that Hall's decision to
marry Martha may have been a matter of indifference to Kezzy, almost a
relief. She doubted whether she could measure up to his standards, and she
preferred to trust her future to God rather than to Westley Hall.

The Closing Years

There is little more to relate about Kezzy Wesley. After her father died,
her mother went to live, for a time, with her daughter Emily at Gainsborough.
Her mother then went to live with her son, Samuel Wesley, and finally accepted an invitation to stay with the Halls. Kezzy also may have lived for
a short time with Samuel and then accepted the invitation of the Halls, much
to the anger and fury of her three brothers. Nevertheless, she seems to have
been happy with the Halls, and after her mother joined the family her life
seems to have gone along smoothly.

John Wesley looked into Kezzy's situation immediately upon his return
from Georgia. He made arrangements for her to stay with the Rev. Henry
Piers, vicar of Bexley. These years proved to be among the happiest of her
life. She made friends of the Gambolds. The Rev. Mr. Gambold had been
a member of the Holy Club formed at Oxford by John and Charles Wesley.

Charles visited Kezzy often and, on one occasion at least, spoke to Kezzy
about her spiritual condition. Kezzy wept freely, put her arms around her
brother Charles and begged him to pray for her. He read to her Mr. Law's
account of redemption and convinced her pretty well that most of her misery
stemmed from her not loving God sufficiently.

How he came to this brilliant deduction is not known, but it proved helpful
to Kezzy who, at this point in her life, needed the assurance that the future
would be better than the past, especially since she now felt herself to be in
full accord with the love and will of God.

After Charles returned to London he wrote a letter of spiritual instruction to his sister, who replied:

> If you can still have patience, and retain any love and tenderness for "a weak, entangled, wretched thing" you may, by your prayers and direction, add much to the happiness of your sincere friend and affectionate sister. (Stev, p. 424)

In the year 1738 Charles and John had both met Peter Boehler who explained to them the Moravian meaning of justifying faith. About this time Charles became seriously ill, and Kezzy came down from Bexley to take care of her brother. For about a week Charles was dangerously ill and near death. Kezzy proved a faithful nurse, pouring out all her love and affection for her brother along with her healing ministry. Charles recovered, but Kezzy became seriously ill. During her period of recovery she and Charles received the Holy Communion each day, and Charles wrote hymns about his recovery, which he and his sister sang together.

In May of that year Charles experienced what has been termed his conversion experience when he laid hold of the idea of justifying faith as the means of salvation. John enjoyed his so-called "heart-warming" experience some days later. Kezzy, however, had returned home and then had gone to the Gambolds at Stanton Harcourt for a visit. Charles met her there and began to explain and press upon her the need for justifying faith for salvation. Kezzy became somewhat distressed and angry, claiming that she already possessed sufficient faith for salvation. She told Charles, "Well, you will know in the next world whether I have faith or no!"

On this Charles asked her, "Will you then discharge me in the sight of God from speaking to you again? If you will, I promise never more to open my mouth till we meet in eternity."

This was too much for Kezzy, who immediately began to cry, and Charles began praying for her. (Stev, p. 425)

During the next two years the two met as often as the public duties of Charles permitted. They became as close to each other as John had been to Martha and Emily. Kezia probably laid hold of a similar faith to that of Charles, although there is no record of what the early Methodists would have called her conversion experience.

She had always been ill, and at thirty-two years of age she died. There is reason for believing that she may have been courted by an unknown suitor sometime before her death, but little is known of the affair. Charles apparently was the only member of the family with her when she died, and he noted in his Journal:

> March 10th, 1741 — Yesterday morning sister Kezzy died in the Lord Jesus. He finished His work, and cut it short for mercy. Full of thankfulness, resignation, and love, without pain or trouble, she commended her spirit into the hands of Jesus, and fell asleep. (Stev, p. 426)

Thus came to an end the quest of the seventh sister for love.

Chapter Nine

Epilogue

The story of the Wesleys and especially the stories of the seven sisters in search of love must be read in the light of the century in which they lived. However, we must be careful that we do not give away the case for Christianity, women's rights, decency in human relations and other beliefs, on the ground that these ideas must be adjusted to the mores of the time in which they are applied.

For example, we can understand the attitude of Susanna and Samuel Wesley toward their daughter Hetty in the light of the moral code of the middle classes of the eighteenth century, but we can never condone it. Samuel had preached often and strongly against loose living, which he considered was typified by Hetty's conduct. We have noted how he ushered out of his house a woman whose open immorality was a stench to his soul. It is hardly to be expected that, with his sense of justice, he could or would treat his daughter any differently than he treated strangers or the members of his parish. In addition, since he had once been sufficiently fond of his daughter to himself provide her with a classical education, her defiance of God's law and her father's will would, in his eyes, have been inexcusable. All this and more we must take into consideration when we judge his action.

However, the fact still remains that Christianity centers on love and the willingness to forgive sins, two essentials, the lack of which can keep a so-called Christian out of the Kingdom of Heaven. There is a universal quality about Christianity and its beliefs that rises above the mores of any generation. Regardless of the time and the existing attitude of the middle classes towards erring daughters, Susanna and Samuel, who professed to be Christians, should have seen Hetty's fault, as well as the faults of their parishoners, through the eyes of love and forgiveness.

Samuel and Susanna excused themselves on the ground that they doubted the sincerity of Hetty's repentance. They, thereby, made themselves judges of the human spirit, of which only God can be the judge.

It should be recalled that Susanna may have paid a heavy price for what may be called the dichotomy of her soul. At least one authority, Mrs. Nolan Harmon, attributes Susanna's serious illness to the conflict within her between her conscience and what she thought was fitting and right.

Fundamentally, both Susanna and Samuel, Sr. seemed to lack the spirit of love. As much as one may admire the stalwart qualities and abilities of Susanna Wesley, and as much as one may appreciate the scholarship and the ministerial leadership of Samuel, one cannot help but feel that both lacked that warmth of love and human understanding which recreates and saves.

111

In her old age Susanna came nearer to a living expression of love than at any time in her life. This irritated John Wesley who, by this time, had become a martinet in his relationship with his preachers and his people. In his sermon on *The Education of Children* he wrote, "In fourscore years I have never met with one woman who knew how to manage grandchildren. My own mother, who governed her children so well, could never govern one grandchild."

Susanna had reached the place where she was enjoying her children or, in this case, grandchildren; where she saw that it was more important to have a loving relationship with a child than a disciplinary attitude. In her own household, of course, she had needed that order which could only come about by making her own will paramount. She had insisted on "breaking the will" of the child, whatever that may mean, but in all her wise advice on the rearing of children she never once spoke of the necessity of demonstrating love and affection for them. Samuel, of course, never came near to this goal. He was proud of his sons, and, in his way, appreciated his daughters, but love in its warmest, deepest sense was foreign to his character.

This is a sad fact about the Wesley family and gives one pause in extolling the virtues of parents who seemed to lack one of the central virtues of Christianity. This, of course, is a form of Methodist heresy, and I may be overstating the case; but my point is that Christianity is a universal religion with universal absolutes of which one is love and another the forgiveness of sins, and if Christianity is to have meaning for any generation, it must have those meanings, at least, for every generation. Its central precepts and teachings cannot be adjusted to the mores of any particular time or place. Therefore, although we may understand the conduct of the Wesleys in their relationship with Hetty, we can never condone or excuse it, lest we give away the whole case for Christianity.

Another observation is that the story of the Wesley sisters demonstrates how far we have come in defending those rights which naturally belong to women but which have for generations been submerged by men. Unfortunately, Christianity itself, while through its history it has done a great deal for womens' rights, has also held women in strict bondage; and whenever it has granted a particular right to women, it has, all too often, done so as a monarch granting a gift rather than as a judge enforcing justice.

In the present day we may be in danger of pushing matters too far and eventually creating a matriarchal society, but, for the moment, that is only a remote possibility. Much remains to be done to restore all natural rights to women, and the story of the Wesley sisters emphasizes how miserable the condition of women can become when these rights are forceably withheld.

Another fact that is clearly demonstrated through the *Seven Sisters in Search of Love* is the vindication of the statement of St. Augustine, "Thou hast made us for Thyself, and we are restless till we find our rest in thee."

Each of the sisters sought for human love, each longed to love and be loved. Mary and Anne came nearest to this goal, but all the sisters eventually came to the place where they rested their case in God and sought to be sheltered by His enfolding arms. This, of course, sounds more like a sentimental rather than a theological conclusion. It would certainly have had the approval of Charles Wesley, who wrote "Jesus Lover of My Soul," but it would have irritated John, who dropped his brother's hymn from his important hymnal for the Methodists in 1780.

However, in this day of uncertainty, cruelty, starvation and the fear of total destruction through nuclear warfare, society might once more be in need of the truth learned by the seven Wesley sisters in search of love.

A final observation is that the Wesleys were indeed a most unusual family, and the world would be a far poorer place without their lives and their stories. A family that can produce two men of genius like John and Charles Wesley, a scholar of the stature of Samuel Wesley, Jr., and seven daughters whose minds were little less brilliant must be admired and, where possible, emulated.

Additional Books Consulted

Banks, John. *Nancy, Nancy.* Penwork (Leeds) Ltd., 1984.

Clarke, Eliza. *Eminent Women Series: Susanna Wesley,* Ed. John H. Ingram, 2nd ed., London: W. H. Allen & Co., 1890.

Edwards, Maldwyn. *My Dear Sister.* Penwork (Leeds) Ltd., N.D.

Hampson, John. *Memoirs of the Late Rev. John Wesley,* 3 vols. Sunderland: James Graham, 1791.

Heitzenrater, Richard P. *The Elusive Mr. Wesley.* 2 vols. Nashville: Abingdon Press, 1984.

Kirk, John. *The Mother of the Wesleys.* Cincinnati: Poe and Hitchcock, 1867.

Lee, Umphrey. *The Lord's Horseman.* New York, London: The Century Co., 1928.

Leckey, W.E.H.A. *A History of England in the Eighteenth Century.* 8 vols. New York: D. Appleton and Co., 1879.

Marshall, Dorothy. *Eighteenth Century England.* London: Longman's, 1962.

McConnell, Francis J. *John Wesley.* New York, Cincinnati, Chicago: The Abingdon Press, 1939.

Moore, The Rev. Henry. *The Life of The Rev. John Wesley.* 2 vols. New York: N. Bangs and J. Emory, 1825.

Outler, Albert C. *John Wesley.* New York: Oxford University Press, 1964.

Priestly, Joseph. *Original Letters by the Rev. John Wesley and His Friends.* Birmingham, England: Thomas Pearson, 1791.

Quiller-Couch, A. T. *Hetty Wesley.* London: The Amalgamated Press, Ltd., N. D.

Southey, Robert. *The Life of Wesley and Rise and Progress of Methodism.* 2 vols. Third Edition, Notes by S. T. Coleridge, Edited by The Rev. Charles Cuthbert Southey. London: Longman, Brown, Green and Longman, 1846.

Schmidt, Martin. *John Wesley A Theological Biography.* 3 vols. Translated by Norman P. Goldhawk. New York, Nashville: Abingdon Press, 1962-1973.

Stephen, Leslie. *English Literature and Society in the Eighteenth Century.* Ford Lectures. New York: G. P. Putnam's Sons, 1907.

Stephen, Leslie. *History of English Thought in the Eighteenth Century.* 2 vols. London: Smith, Elder & Co., 1876.

Turberville, A. S. *Johnson's England.* Oxford: Clarendon Press, 1933.

Tyerman, Luke. *The Life and Times of the Rev. John Wesley.* 3 vols. New York: Harper and Brothers, 1872.

For a full account of the dates of the births, baptisms, etc. of the Wesley family see article by Frank Baker in *Methodist History* entitled "Investigating Wesley Family Traditions," Vol. XXVI, No. 3, April 1988, p. 154ff.

INDEXES
Persons

Annesley, Samuel (Brother of Mrs. Samuel Wesley, Sr.), his strange life and disappearance, 31; promises handsome present to his niece Susanna, 31; promise not fulfilled, 31

Baker, Frank, 10, 31
Barry, James, 14, 105
Betty, Miss. (Friend of John Whitelamb and sister of Sally Lumley) 43, 44
Blackwell, Ebenezer, 35
Blake, William, 71
Boehler, Peter, 110
Boswell, James, 5, 6, 79, 96, 97, 99
Bray, Mr., 78
Buckingham, Duke of, 102
Butterfield, Mr., 36

Castleton, Earl of, incident with Samuel Wesley, Sr., 4
Clarendon, Lord, 23
Clark, Adam, his appraisal of Mary or "Molly" Wesley, 39; his appraisal of Mehetabel or "Hetty" Wesley, 51; gathers some of "Hetty's" poems, 71. M. 11, 73, 79, 95
Clarke, Eliza, 96
Clayton, John (a member of the Holy Club) questions Westley Hall about his proposed marriage and his view on celibacy, 88

De Maupassant, Guy, 51
Dickens, Charles, 51

Edwards, Maldwyn, 11, 98
Ellison, Richard, married Susanna or "Sukey" Wesley, 31; abuses his wife, 32ff; house destroyed by fire, 34; wife deserts him, 34; his strange attempt at reconciliation, 35; lands ruined by floods, 35; receives financial aid through John Wesley, 35; becomes a Methodist, 36; closing years and death, 36. M. 105
Ellison, Mrs. Richard—see Wesley, Susanna or "Sukey"

Gambold, John (A member of the Holy Club) 43, 109, 110
Garrick, David (18th century English actor) 85
Gaunt, Ann (Daughter of Susanna or "Sukey" Wesley) 36

Grantham, Mr. and Mrs. of Kelstein, Mehetabel or "Hetty" serves as governess for 56, 57; Martha or "Patty" serves as governess for and companion to, 82. M. 6
Green, V. H. H., untenable theory concerning the Wesley sisters, 56, 57. M. 11
Greenaway, Elizabeth, 94.

Hall, Westley, background, 86; refuses a parish, 86; proposes to Martha or "Patty" Wesley and is accepted, 87; his courtship of Kezia or "Kezzy" Wesley (see under Wesley, Kezia) reveals to John Wesley letters from John Whitelamb condemning Kezia, 88, 89; marries Martha or "Patty" Wesley, 89; deserts his wife, 93, 94; his various affairs (sexual) 94, 95; becomes a polygamist, 95; goes to the West Indies, 96; returns to London, 96; later life and death, 97. M. 81, 97, 107, 108, 109.
Hall, Mrs. Westley—see Wesley, Martha or "Patty."
Harmon, Mrs. Nolan or Rebecca Lamar, 11, 56, 68, 111.
Harper, Robert, marries Emilia or "Emily" Wesley, 25; mistreats his wife, 25; theory that he absconded with her money, 25; probable death of, 15. M. 29
Harper, Mrs. Robert —see Wesley, Emilia or "Emily."
Harry (Manservant of the Wesleys) 52
Hastings, Lady Margaret, 86
Hawthorne, Nathaniel, 51
Haxey, 47, 58
Heitzenrater, Richard P., 10, 41
Horbery, Matthew, marries Mary or "Molly" Wesley to John Whitelamb, 45; his relationship with Martha or "Patty" Wesley with a sketch of his life, 85, 87
Hutton, Mr., 77

Ingham, Benjamin (A member of the Holy Club) in love with Martha or "Patty" Wesley, 86; marries Lady Margaret Hastings; 86. M. 28
Johnson, Mr., courts Martha or "Patty" Wesley, 84, 85; M. 87
Johnson, Samuel (18th century lexicographer) his relationship with Martha or "Patty" Wesley 97ff. M. 1, 4, 5, 7, 79, 80, 97

"Molly," 38, 58; is forced into a loveless marriage, 58; first child born at Louth, 59; makes attempt at reconciliation with her parents, 59; defended by her brother John in a sermon, 60; visits the Lamberts, 61; meets with her mother at the home of the Lamberts, 61; moves to London, 62; renews relationship with her brother Charles, 62; visited by her father, 62, 63; opens a school, 63; writes poem to her husband, 63ff; death of her third child, 66; her fear that the deaths of her babies was caused by her father's refusal to forgive her youthful indiscretion, 66; her later view that the lead fumes from her husband's plumbing shop was the cause of her babies deaths, 66; poetry appears in magazines, 66, 67; lauded by *Silvius* in *The Gentleman's Magazine*, 67; her care for her Uncle Matthew, 68; not present at her father's death, 68; reconciliation with her mother and other members of the family, 68; later years and death, 69, 70; appraisal of her poetry, 71; M. 1, 2, 3, 4, 21, 38, 39, 51ff, 82, 83, 111, 112

Wesley, Samuel, Jr., writes poem about his sisters, 15; helps supply a gown for John Whitelamb, 42; desires reconciliation between his parents and Mehetabel or "Hetty," 62; writes poem on marriage of his sister Anne or "Nancy," 74; displeasure with John Lambert, Anne's husband, 75; cuts off correspondence with Kezia or "Kezzy," 90; M. 12, 13, 19, 20, 22, 26, 30, 31, 32, 33, 34, 49, 51, 58, 59, 60, 63, 72, 89, 106, 109

Wesley, Mrs. Samuel, Jr., 20, 59, 62, 67, 81

Wesley, Samuel, Sr., aids in teaching children, 2; checks bedtimes of his oldest daughters, 2; attitude toward Old Jeffrey, 2; serves as Chaplain at sea, 4; marriage in London, 4; stationed at South Ormsby, 4; incident with Marquis of Normanby, 4; expresses affection for his sons, 9; his opinion of Richard Ellison, 32; commends Mary or "Molly" for her industry, 39, 40; life saved by John Whitelamb, 42; writes to Lord Chancellor to secure Whitelamb's appointment to Wroot, 46; death, 68; M. 1, 8, 9, 12, 13, 24, 30, 39, 41, 43, 51, 52, 56, 57, 58, 59, 60, 66, 67, 73, 88, 111, 112

Wesley, Sarah (Daughter of Charles and niece to the Wesley sisters and brothers) 96, 100

Wesley, Susanna (Wife of Samuel Wesley, Sr.)

method for educating her children, 2; lists the virtues, 9; her rejection of a close relationship with John, 9; her opinion of Richard Ellison, 32; her attitude toward John Whitelamb, 43ff; her letter about Whitelamb, 45; her letter recording her meeting with Mehetabel or "Hetty" at the home of the Lamberts, 61; her later reconciliation with "Hetty," 68; her so-called conversion under the administration of Westley Hall, 91; death, 92; M. 1, 2, 4, 8, 9, 12, 13, 14, 28, 30, 31, 43, 44, 51, 58, 60, 74, 76, 86, 91, 102, 111, 112.

Wesley, Susanna (Who died shortly after her birth) 12

Wesley, Susanna or "Sukey," birth, 13; appearance and personal endowments, 30; her description of Old Jeffrey, 31; lives with her Uncle Annesley, 31; her disappointment at failing to receive gift promised by her uncle, 32; marries Richard Ellison, 32; abused by her husband, 33ff; her children, 34; a possible trip to Georgia, 34; fire destroys her home, 34; she deserts her husband, 34; rejects her husband's attempt at reconciliation, 35; later years and death, 36; M. 21, 22, 30, 83, 105, 106

Whitehart, Ruth, 95

Whitefield (George) 28

Whitelamb, John, birth, appearance and education, 40; serves as amanuensis for Samuel Wesley, Sr., 41; his troubled existence in the Wesley household, 41; falls in love with Mary or "Molly" Wesley, 41; saves life of Samuel Wesley, Sr., 42; educated at Oxford, 42; his poverty and need for a gown, 42; his affair with Miss Betty, 43, 44; marries "Molly" Wesley, 43; assigned to parish at Wroot, 46; death of his wife in childbirth, 47; later life and death, 48, 49; John Wesley's belated interest in Whitelamb, 49. M. 88

Whitelamb, Mrs. John—*see* Wesley, Mary or "Molly."

Woodhouse, Mrs. 49

Wright, Amelia (Daughter of William Wright and Mehetabel or "Hetty" Wesley) 68

Wright, William, marries Mehetabel or "Hetty" Wesley, 58; occupation, 59; abuses his wife, 63; later life and death, 70; M. 61, 62, 63, 65, 66, 69, 70, 75, 76, 77

Wright, Mrs. William, see Wesley, Mehetabel or "Hetty."

INDEXES
Places

INDEXES
Subjects